THE
Mistletoe Bluff

Also by Emily Schneider

THE
Mistletoe Bluff

EMILY SCHNEIDER

MAGIC KEEPERS PRESS

The Mistletoe Bluff

For information contact:
Magic Keepers Press, LLC
magickeeperspress.com

Paperback: 979-8-9881156-2-5

Ebook: 979-8-9881156-1-8

First edition December 2023.

Edited by Oak Moss Editorial LLC
Proofreading by Brittany Cox
Cover Design by Ink & Laurel © 2023

*For those who feel easily forgotten,
or like they're everyone's last choice:
I see you.
You are important.
You are loved.*

PROLOGUE

Maya

One Year Ago

I never thought I'd be here—my entire future hinging on a silly little competition—yet here I was.

Well, *entire* future might have been a slight exaggeration, but I was going with it.

The professor stood at the front of the room behind a wooden podium holding a tiny little trophy that looked like it had been picked up at a dollar store. The classroom reminded me of a science lab. There were several long rectangular tables, each one covered in various cameras, tripods, lenses, lighting kits, and other related doohickeys.

The overhead fluorescent lighting pounded into my skull, and my hands were slick with sweat as I clasped them together, praying and wishing with all my might that my name would be called.

This was huge. This was my chance. It might have been a small, local college competition, but it came with big strings attached.

"The two finalists in the Meridel Community College photography competition and a chance at a two-page spread in the *Iowa Artist Gazette* are..." Professor Wellotto paused and glanced around the classroom.

A breath shuddered out of me. The *Iowa Artist Gazette* was a huge magazine that was sent statewide to thousands of consumers, with pages upon pages of up-and-coming artists and photographers. It had the power to rocket my business, Sunflower Fields Photography, from nothing to *something*.

The giant clock ticking away over the door lit a fuse on my nerves. A headache formed at my temples, and my eye twitched from the stress.

"Oliver Lewis!" The professor declared. My heartbeat stuttered in my chest before resuming its pounding.

I glared over my shoulder at my archnemesis—the British guy who had upended every chance at winning I ever had. He threw a smug smile over his shoulder as he passed me, his blue eyes flashing behind thick-framed Clark Kent glasses, and my blood burned beneath my skin at his smugness.

Unlike Clark Kent, Oliver Lewis was no superhero in disguise. He was the evil villain, hands down. He was the Lex Luthor to my Superman—err, Supergirl? Whatever, my point remained.

Each project we were assigned in class was a mini competition. Whoever won each assignment amassed points toward the final prize at the end of the year—the spread in the magazine.

But that blasted Brit had outranked me in far too many assignments—and always by a few measly points. Last I checked, we were neck and neck. Though Professor Wellotto hadn't posted points in a couple weeks, so I had no idea where we stood now.

The one thing all semester that I had won by a landslide was my photoshoot with my best friend, Elsie, and my cousin, Jameson. Nothing topped a couple's photoshoot between two strangers—especially when their chemistry had been so far off the charts, they made their own chart. Those photos were some of my best works, and for once they had outshined Oliver and his weird photoshoot of a couple in corn costumes. Yep, that's right. The professor had given us an assignment to do a *unique* photoshoot, and his grand idea was for them to dress up as corn.

I fought the urge to groan as he walked to the front of the room, his gait lazy and slow, hands shoved in his pockets, and head held high like he owned the world. I wanted to slap that irritating smirk right off his face.

Why was Oliver even here in Meridel, Iowa of all places? Didn't he have bigger and better things happening over in England? Wasn't there anyone else's life he could go ruin? My spiraling, blood-boiling thoughts over my classmate careened to a halt as Professor Wellotto's voice cut through the silence.

"And Maya Beck!"

I blinked at the professor. It took a second too long for her words to register.

Her long silver hair shifted over her shoulder as she cocked her head at me. She waved her hand for me to come forward. "That's you, Maya. You're the second finalist. Please come join Mr. Lewis at the front."

Even though I had hoped to be named a finalist, it still caught me off guard, especially when luck seemed to fall on everyone but me.

On shaking legs, I pushed to my feet, trying to infuse confidence into each movement, wishing this competition didn't mean so much to me. While my photos from *The Heart Shot* photoshoot had gained some traction in the local community, bringing me a small influx of inquiries, it hadn't lasted long enough. Within a few months, I was back to broke Maya, in debt Maya, who desperately needed a lucky break.

This spread in the *Iowa Artist Gazette* was my ticket to finally pay off some of my debt, to *finally* have some stability for the first time in my life, and, not to mention, making a name for myself in the photography community.

I lifted my chin higher as I walked up to join Oliver.

As I passed him, avoiding eye contact at all costs, the slimy booger of a man slid his boot out just enough so that my foot caught, and I stumbled forward with a small yelp. My ankle twisted, which landed me right in Oliver's arms. His warm hands went around my waist, and my own slammed into his chest. Of course, the muscle there was rock hard, and I shoved down the urge to punch it just to see if it hurt him.

A whiff of his sweet but smoky scent—like vanilla mixed with pipe tobacco—smothered my senses. I clenched my jaw. My skin burned beneath my clothes where his hands held me tight, his touch blazing through my layers. Our faces were inches apart. His blue eyes flickered with some emotion I couldn't place as he held me captive with his gaze. There was a faint ring of gold around each iris that I had never cared to notice before.

Oliver's breath tickled my neck, and his short beard scratched my ear as he crooned, "Should we add *clumsy* to your list of class achievements, Maya? Or were you just dying to be in my arms?" His low voice combined with his accent had my insides twisting.

"I never wanted to be in *your* arms," I spat, ripping myself out of his hold, and taking a giant step to the side. Some of the class stared at us, most of them with drooping eyelids, while others ignored us and scrolled on their phones instead. I found myself thankful that none of them seemed to notice, or care about our interaction—or how red my face probably was now.

Oliver smirked as I smoothed down my hair and put as many inches between us as possible. And, of course, the moment I dared to look at him he had the audacity to wink at me. I clenched my hands into fists at my sides.

Don't punch him, Maya. It's not worth it. Then you really won't win.

I was sure there was some rule that would disqualify me if I got into a physical altercation with another contestant, and I definitely couldn't afford *that*.

What was with this man? Every time I saw him, he went out of his way to bug me. Whether it was teasing me like we were two kids in elementary school or looking over my shoulder at whatever I was working on—which I despised—or just generally being a turd, like just now with his tripping stunt. One time I had my hair in a topknot, and every time he'd pass by, he'd either swat it or squeeze it, like he couldn't resist his inner childlike tendencies.

He never bothered our other classmates, and I swear from the first moment we met, he had decided to make it his life mission to annoy me. I wasn't sure we had even had a full conversation the entire semester because any time we did talk, it consisted of him taunting me, then me telling him to shove it, and then him laughing and walking away.

I loathed Oliver Lewis.

I took a deep, calming breath, forcing my muscles to relax. I pushed a small smile to my lips with enormous effort and looked at Professor Wellotto.

She studied Oliver and I for a moment before turning to face the class. "As a reminder, the winner of this competition will receive an exclusive two-page spread in the *Iowa Artist Gazette*, thereby having thousands of eyes on your photos. It's a great honor, not to mention a potential career starter." The professor paused. She swallowed, her throat making a sucking noise, letting the anticipation build for another moment.

This was it. Meridel had proved to be far too small to grow my business, and this was my last shot at making it here. *Come on, please say my name.*

"And the winner of the Meridel Community College photography competition is…"

The other six people in the room had their chins in their hands or rested their heads on their arms, not caring in the slightest about who won. I was pretty sure the guy in the back row, who I nicknamed Fabio thanks to his long blonde hair, was drooling all over the table as he slept on his textbook.

No one else cared about this, but I did. This was everything to me.

My fingers tingled at my sides, and I forced my attention back on the professor, willing her to say my name instead of Oliver's.

Sweat pooled on my low back, and I held my arms together against my sides, hoping I didn't have pit stains that would show my nerves. The clock over the door still ticked away, each beat like the blow of a hammer to my heart.

"Oliver Lewis!" The class flinched at how loud

the professor's declaration was before they gave a halfhearted applause.

All the air escaped my lungs in a whoosh. My stomach fell through my feet, through the three stories of the building, through concrete, dirt, grass, and earth, squashing and shattering into a million tiny pieces.

The sides of my vision went blurry, and I couldn't bring myself to watch as Oliver stepped forward to shake the professor's hand, nor could I look at the infernal smirk I imagined was on his face when he turned back to me, ridiculous tiny trophy in hand.

I lost. My chest caved in, my arms wrapping around my stomach. I stared at my feet and bit the inside of my cheek, trying to keep the burning in my eyes at bay. There went the opportunity to grow my photography career. There went my chance at paying off my debt. There went a chance at stability for the first time ever.

A pair of shiny black boots appeared in front of me, and anger burned like a roaring inferno in my gut as I looked up to find Oliver's smug face staring at me.

"No hard feelings, Maya?" he asked, extending his hand. His eyes flickered with amusement. I couldn't decide if his accent made the comment better or worse.

"That would imply I had any feelings about you to begin with. Which I don't," I snapped, slapping his hand away before heading to the table to grab my coat and flee the campus.

Strong fingers encircled my bicep, stopping me in

my tracks.

"Maya." Oliver moved in front of me, stepping way too close for my current anger level to handle.

I pried his hand off my arm and glared up at him. "Don't touch me." My eyes filled with traitorous tears, but I refused to give him the satisfaction of seeing me cry. "You've already taken enough from me in this class," I said, fixing my eyes on his chest, unable to look in his blue eyes any longer. "Just let me leave with some measure of dignity intact now that we never have to see each other again."

Oliver stilled, those ice-blue eyes softening behind his glasses, before moving out of my way. I grabbed my backpack, swung it over my shoulder and made for the door when he stepped in front of me again. My sneakers squeaked on the floor as I stopped.

"Maya, I—"

I groaned, cutting him off. "What don't you understand, Oliver? Leave. Me. Alone."

Oliver's brows lowered over his eyes as he studied me. "Is that really what you want, Maya?"

"Yes."

Without another word, I stalked out of the classroom muttering, "I never want to see you again," and left Oliver Lewis behind once and for all.

Oliver

Coffee was supposed to fix everything.

Spoiler alert: the coffee wasn't doing anything for me except making my heart race.

I glared at the drips of condensation sliding down my iced Americano as I sat at The Roasted Bean. My laptop was open on the table, taunting me that I hadn't accomplished anything in the last two hours I'd been here.

I hoped the caffeine would help me focus on editing the photos from the last shoot I did before I left London a few days ago, but so far, my mind had only been spinning in circles.

Namely, around a girl I was struggling to get out of my head. A girl who just happened to live here in

Meridel. A girl who hated me.

I looked out the window. Light snow fell outside, white flakes dancing in little flurries on their way to the ground. Jazzy Christmas music tinkled through the speakers.

I thought about heading back to my townhouse and seeing if that would help me accomplish *something*, but after living in the busyness of London my entire life, I wasn't quite used to the silence and isolation at home. I loved the slower pace of this small town, but it had been an adjustment to not have chaos and noise as my constant companion.

I needed to finish editing these photos so I could officially take my break from the agency, but as the last of my coffee slurped up the straw and into my mouth, I knew today was not that day. I considered buying another drink, the tantalizing scent of espresso in the air made my mouth water, but my heart was already *thump-thumping* harder than it needed to.

Maybe I should just go home.

With a sigh, I closed my laptop, packed up my bag, and left the coffee shop. The sidewalk was slick beneath my boots as I made my way back to my Jeep. I crawled inside, letting out a breath of relief as the seat warmers came to life.

Maybe a drive around Meridel would clear my head enough to let me focus.

If nothing else, it'll let me keep procrastinating.

The streets of Meridel, a small town on the western edge of Iowa, were decked out with Christmas lights, which dangled between lamp posts across the road, and giant wreaths hung on each side. Shop owners were out shoveling the sidewalks in front of their stores, trying in vain to keep up with the Midwest winter. At the end of Main Street, I turned right on a dirt road that led out of town. I didn't know where I was going, only that I needed to keep driving.

My phone pinged in the cupholder, and I glanced down, the name *Dad* flashing across the screen. Pressing the button that would have the text read aloud, I braced myself for whatever my father had to say.

DAD

Have you entered the contest yet?

A surge of anger bubbled in my stomach.

I had been avoiding my father, and this question, for weeks now.

No, I hadn't entered, nor did I plan on it. He didn't want me to enter the contest because he thought I deserved to win. No, he wanted me to enter because *if* I won, it would bring endless exposure to his company—the one I worked for.

His agency employed dozens of photographers in London. Many of them excelled at different types of photos, such as retail, real estate, or family photos. I, unfortunately, was its "shining star," able to do well at any of them, which my dad never wasted an opportunity to exploit.

My award-winning photography was the reason for the exposure and success he'd had thus far. I was a bargaining chip in board meetings, and he knew how to play me like a fiddle to get me to agree to gigs I never wanted to do.

Our conversations over the past few years had been strained at best since I had started speaking up and telling him *no,* and he never missed an opportunity to tell me how disappointed he was in me.

I enjoyed photography, but I didn't want to be my dad. I wanted to make a difference; for my art to mean something. I was so used to viewing everyone else as my competition or trying to make myself stand out, and I hated it. I didn't want something I loved to be tainted by a need to be seen.

For years, my father had used me and my talent to further his company and career, and after I won the spread in the *Iowa Artist Gazette,* I gained a lot of new clients in the States, which had been a goal of my father's—to take the agency international—so, of course, that made things even more tense between us. He saw only my talent, not the man behind the camera, not his son. I'd had enough.

Hence the indefinite break I was taking...right after I finished editing those photos.

Determination flooded through me. I deleted his text

without a response and turned onto the next road that would lead to my house. A few moments later, the trees to the right opened up to an enormous snow-covered field, one which boasted giant sunflowers in the fall.

A familiar car was parked in a tiny lot on the side of the road.

I pulled over, my limbs on autopilot, and into the spot next to the Honda Accord, the one that I had parked next to enough times at Meridel Community College to be certain who it belonged to. I wasn't sure why I thought it would be a good idea when the owner of that car had flat out told me to stay away from her.

But when it came to Maya Beck, all my good sense disappeared.

The frigid winter air seeped into my layers as I stepped out of my Jeep and stood between our cars. Across the field, a familiar girl was crouched in the snow, her blonde hair peeking out from beneath a black beanie. Maya's back faced me as she photographed a couple rolling in the snow in the distance.

I wanted to call out to her, wanted to see those blue eyes and try to make her smile, but the face she made when she told me she didn't want to see me again flickered in my mind and froze my feet to the earth.

For some reason, Maya hated me, and I despised it because I had had a massive crush on her since the first day I met her. I had signed up for that photography class on a whim to continue improving my skills, but I hadn't counted on meeting a beautiful woman that made my heart stutter whenever I saw her.

She was talented and determined—I had never seen someone light up the way she did behind a camera—and her quick comebacks whenever I teased her made her even more endearing. Maya was whip smart and I loved it.

And that last day of our class, when I had *accidentally* tripped her, and she ended up falling in my arms...I couldn't get the feel of her in my embrace out of my head.

Oh, and up until recently, I lived in England too. That always put a damper on relationships. No one enjoyed the whole long-distance thing.

I hadn't had any interactions with her since she told me to leave her alone when the class was over. Heck, I'd never had any actual conversations with her at all aside from when I teased her. I couldn't help it...it was too much fun to push her buttons.

And, if I were honest with myself, I wasn't the best at talking to people unless I was behind a camera. It was another unfortunate side effect of being under my father's thumb for too long, forcing me to see people as rivals when they weren't. That, *unfortunately*, translated into teasing and bothering Maya when all I wanted to do was talk to her.

Never did I imagine it all would end in her hating me, though.

The falling snow and the cold faded into the background as I stood there watching her. All I could focus on was Maya and how much I missed seeing her face after spending the last few months back in England.

I had followed her social media accounts for a while—with her skill in photography, who wouldn't? But for some reason she quit posting weeks ago, and I was dying to know how she was doing.

As much as I wanted to get to know that brilliant, smart, gorgeous woman hiding in the field, I also didn't want to disrespect her wishes or make her uncomfortable.

With a sigh, I turned to climb back in my Jeep and my boots slipped on a patch of ice. I slid forward, struggling to get my feet under me, and fell against her car door, the metal button on my coat squished between my body and the car.

It made a horrendous squealing noise as I continued to slip on the ice and tried in vain to stop sliding around. When the ice finally had mercy on me, and I was able to stand without further slippage, my stomach gave a mighty lurch at the sight of the damage I'd caused.

The good news: I didn't fall on my bum.

The bad news: Maya's car had broken my fall.

My chest squeezed. This was the last thing I needed, another reason for Maya to hate me. I ran my gloved hands over my coat, thinking. What was I supposed to do? Should I face Maya and apologize? Or did I take the coward's way out and make a run for it?

As much as I wished to see her again, this wasn't how I wanted to do it.

I opened the door to my Jeep and searched the interior for anything I could use. A white napkin stuck out of the side of the center console, and I snatched it, followed by a pen, and wrote a quick note. I tried to keep it short and concise, not wanting to give away that it was me until I needed to.

I scribbled my number at the bottom and then stared at the white scrap in my hands. I was a coward to run away, but at least I offered to pay for the scratch. That was still the responsible thing to do, right? Maybe adding a happy Christmas sentiment would ease the blow.

I winced. *Probably not.*

Running a hand over my face, I blew out a breath, then shoved the napkin onto her windshield.

As I crawled back into my Jeep, sparing a glance at Maya who was none the wiser to what I had done, I pulled away from the field feeling like the worst sort of person.

I left a ridiculous note on a napkin and shoved it under her windshield wiper.

Then fled the scene of the crime.

Please don't hate me, Maya.

Surely, she'd call me, want me to pay to have the car doors fixed. Any sane person would…right? I could only imagine what her reaction would be when she found out I was the one to damage her car.

A shaky breath worked its way out of me, and I banged my head against the headrest as I drove through the snowy roads toward my townhouse.

This was not how I pictured spending Christmas in Meridel.

Maya

"That'll be two thousand dollars."

My jaw hit the floor. "Excuse me?"

The smell of car oil permeated the small auto body shop as I stood gaping at the man behind the counter. He blinked at me, his eyes half closed, as if he were moments from falling asleep. He lifted the trucker hat off his forehead long enough to scratch his greasy head before wiggling it back down, looking at me with narrowed eyes and flattened lips that said *I don't want to deal with dumb women in my shop anymore.*

"Two thousand dollars. To fix the scratch on your car." He drew out the words, as if he were speaking to a child who didn't understand that one plus one equaled two.

I glanced around, expecting some reality TV show host to jump out and tell me I'd been punked or something. I looked over my shoulder to find two people waiting behind me, a man who was engrossed in his phone, and an older woman who looked at me with eyes full of pity.

I turned back to cranky auto-shop man. "B-b-but Google said it would only be a couple hundred bucks," I stammered.

The man rolled his eyes. "Well, Google won't be doing the repairs on your car, and this is no surface-level scratch. It's deep into the paint, all the way to the metal, and will rust from exposure to the elements by the way, which requires a lot more work. Therefore, two thousand dollars. Now, I'll either need you to make the appointment or leave as I have other customers to attend to." He gave a vague wave to the people waiting.

Nausea filled my stomach. My credit card was maxed out and I had approximately forty-six dollars, give or take a few cents, in my bank account.

"Look..." I leaned forward, looking at the guy's nametag. "Paul, I don't have that kind of money. Isn't there anything you can do? Maybe a payment plan or something?"

Paul rolled his eyes again, pointing to the sign hanging behind him that said, "We don't offer payment plans. Payment required in full."

Dang it.

I clenched my fists to keep from punching his face.

That definitely wouldn't do me any favors.

"We don't do payment plans, lady. We require payment in full before service is done," he snipped, regurgitating the sign. "That's the policy. If you can't afford it, then step aside."

Rude.

"Fine," I snapped. "I'm leaving. You don't have to be a jerk about it. Merry Christmas." I fought the urge to tack on *ya filthy animal* as I readjusted my purse on my shoulder and stalked out of the shop.

I was feeling just a tad vindicated, like I had put the dude in his place by calling him out for being a jerk at Christmas time, but then my purse caught on the door handle. It would have been less embarrassing if it was a simple snag that required a brief pause to free myself.

But no, the universe was cruel.

Instead, the force of my purse catching on the door flung me backward, landing me on the hard tile, right on my butt.

My teeth sang from the impact, my tailbone likely bruised, but nothing hurt worse than my pride. The lady at the back of the line asked if I was okay as I struggled to stand. I gave the barest of nods before limping through the door, purse clutched tight to my chest. I didn't bother to look back at Paul to see if he cared that I had just butt-planted on his floor.

The winter air smothered me as I stepped outside, eradicating any ounce of warmth left in my body, and

I didn't know what was colder—the weather or Paul's attitude.

A shaky breath pooled in the cold air as I exhaled. I stopped next to my car and dragged my fingers along the scratch on the door. How could something so small cost so much? Sure, it spanned both the front and rear doors, but it wasn't *that* deep. Definitely not two thousand dollars' worth.

What had that infernal scratcher even done? It was too long and distinct to have been an accident. It looked like someone had keyed my car on purpose.

I rested my forehead on the top of the door. I'd never have that kind of money to fix it.

I supposed I should have counted my blessings—it was only a scratch and not something that made the vehicle inoperable. But still...it was an eyesore that wasn't my fault and yet *I* had to pay for it.

Climbing into the car, I let out a frustrated groan before banging my head on the steering wheel. I thought about turning the key to flood the car with some warmth since it was only thirty degrees outside, but I couldn't bring myself to do it. The past year had been such an utter, colossal failure and disappointment.

Aside from succeeding in getting my best friend and my cousin together, which was a feat in itself, nothing else had gone right. Ever since Oliver Lewis won the prize that should have been mine, door after door had slammed in my face. Meridel was too small of a town for me to gain any traction. That magazine spreading the word about Sunflower Fields Photography had been vital.

But Oliver had stolen that opportunity, which left me waitressing at Dina's restaurant on the side, trying to pay off the massive debt I had racked up trying to do something substantial with my life.

And then photographing Jameson proposing to Elsie last week…that was the true kick to my gut. A reminder that I had no promising future in this career, *and* no man.

I let out a long sigh. A Christmas tree air freshener swung from the rearview mirror, but it was so old it didn't smell like anything anymore. Muttering a curse under my breath, wishing something would just work out for once in my life, I went to start the car when something white caught my eye on the passenger seat.

It was the napkin the car scratcher had left on my windshield.

The thing was crumpled in a ball, hiding under my camera bag. I hesitated for a moment before reaching over to dig it out.

It was stiff after getting wet from the snow that day, and I carefully smoothed it against the steering wheel, flinching when I accidentally honked the horn.

Paul would probably think I did it on purpose to spite him, but I wasn't that clever. Though, the mental image of him jumping at the noise and then scowling gave me a bit of satisfaction.

The note on the napkin was hard to read, the handwriting like chicken scratch, and it took several attempts to decipher it.

Sorry about your car, mate! I promise I'll pay for the damages. Give me a call and we can figure things out! Happy Christmas!

The number at the bottom was almost illegible.

The whole reason why I never even considered contacting the person responsible for the damage was because I had a hunch about who it was, and I wanted nothing to do with him.

Oliver Lewis was the only British person in Meridel, Iowa, and definitely the only person who would've written *mate* on that napkin. After the photography class had ended last year, I had heard he went back to England, but was it possible he was back now?

My stomach filled with dread. What would he do to upend my life this time?

But…was it even Oliver? Or was I just being paranoid, jumping to the worst-case scenario?

Only one way to find out, Maya.

I hated being at the mercy of other people. I had learned early in my life not to rely on anyone but myself. I worked hard to be independent, and I despised that I couldn't deal with this car damage by myself. I hated that I was reduced to having to contact my archnemesis to pay for the damage *he* caused—assuming it was him, that is.

Digging my phone out of my coat pocket, I opened a new text thread, entered the phone number, and then…

stared at the screen.

What did I even say? *Hey dude, you ruined my car. You owe me two thousand dollars. Please Venmo me ASAP!*

I rubbed at my temple. No, definitely not that. My fingers hovered over the screen, nails clicking as I painstakingly typed out a message, deleting it at least one hundred times before settling on a final draft.

ME

> Hi. This is the person whose car you scratched and then left a napkin on the window. Seeing as you were the one to damage my car, I think it's only fair you pay for it. Please text me back at your earliest convenience so we can get this sorted out, preferably before Christmas. Thanks.

I didn't bother signing my name because if it *was* Oliver, I didn't want him to know it was me. I didn't need him sabotaging anything else in my life. For all I knew, he'd come back and key the other side of my car just to annoy me some more.

With another sigh, I backed out of the parking lot and turned onto Main Street, heading toward Dina's restaurant and my eight-hour waitressing shift.

One of the things I loved about Meridel was that it was small, most of the businesses fitting on the entirety of Main Street. There was everything from a restaurant and bakery, to a coffee shop, and a little ma and pop grocery store called Wally's Market.

When I was younger, I had only ever wanted to leave Meridel. I wanted to explore new places, take pictures, and live as big as possible.

But that was when life hadn't beaten the joy out of that idea. Before my mom lost her mind after my dad left us, leaving me to fend for myself more often than not. My big dreams shifted into a smaller dream of just surviving, trying to enjoy the small things in each day so I wasn't heartbroken that my great plans for life would never come to pass.

I parked in the back lot at Dina's and hurried inside. Thanks to the holdup at Paul's, I only had two minutes before I needed to clock in. I preferred to be early to everything so that I could ease into it without the anxiety of being late. With a frustrated exhale at how this day had already gone, I slipped into the back and donned my blue apron, sliding a notepad and pen into my pocket and went to work.

Maya

By the time I clocked out of work, it was dark outside, and my stomach was growling something fierce. I grabbed my to-go box of chicken tenders and fries, with a side of fruit because I wasn't *entirely* unhealthy, and made my way out to my car, ready to go home and collapse on the couch with my food and a good old-fashioned holiday rom-com on Hallmark.

My best friend Elsie had gotten me addicted to them two Christmases ago and now I couldn't stop, even if they were unrealistic. Most of the time love didn't happen like that. There was no love at first sight, no mistletoe kisses after fighting your attraction for one another, no house swapping and falling in love with the owner's brother, and definitely no such thing as Christmas magic.

It was all fiction.

But still…I couldn't help but wish for the butterflies and soft smiles and the warm arms of a man to hold me on a cold December night. But I had zero prospects, so Hallmark movies it was. My imagination would have to do for now.

Fresh snow littered the road as I drove home, white knuckling the steering wheel. I despised driving in the snow, and thanks to the poor conditions, it took longer to get to my apartment than usual. By the time I made it inside, my food was cold.

Figures.

Five minutes later, I was spread out on the couch, movie playing on the TV, stuffing my face with glorious fried foods…and a side of fruit. I was so engrossed in the fiery chemistry of the main character and the love interest in the movie that when my phone vibrated on the table next to me, I jumped so high I almost lost the rest of my fries to the floor.

I stared at the phone, half expecting it to grow horns and try to bite me, unable to tap the screen to see if it was the car scratcher. But then another notification came through, lighting the screen up, revealing a text from an unknown number.

With trembling fingers, I picked up the phone and opened the text.

UNKNOWN NUMBER

Hi there. Sorry again about your car. It truly was an accident.

I'm happy to pay for the damage.

I can meet you at the shop to pay for it tomorrow morning.

Does nine work for you?

Well, that was easier than I had expected it to be. I thought for sure the scratcher would be a little weasel and try to get out of paying for it.

I reread the text a few more times. Huh. No use of the word "mate" this time either. The car scratcher also didn't sign a name. I couldn't tell by a toneless text if it was Oliver or not. Maybe I *was* being paranoid. Surely that man wouldn't be back in Meridel of all places when he had all the women of England to bother.

Maybe luck was finally on my side. I typed a quick response, determined not to overthink it.

ME

Nine works for me. I'll meet you at Meridel Auto.

A reply appeared a few seconds later.

UNKNOWN NUMBER

Looking forward to it.

Looking forward to it? What idiot looks forward to forking over a butt-ton of dollars for a car scratch? Not only that but right before Christmas?

I glanced around at my apartment that was devoid of any Christmas decorations. That was the way I liked it. Christmas had always been a hard time, especially after my dad left. My mom always had to work late on Christmas Eve, and then she'd come home and pass out, and I'd spend the rest of Christmas alone. I was lucky if there were any presents under the tree at all.

So now, other than a simple dinner with my cousins, I didn't *do* Christmas, and I certainly didn't spend a stupid amount of money on decor when I had thousands of dollars of debt to pay off.

Thankfully, the last few years Jameson, Emma, and Aunt Maggie had invited me to spend Christmas with them, easing the ache in my chest ever so slightly. But this year, Elsie and Jameson were going to spend the holiday with *her* family instead. Jameson had encouraged Elsie to reconnect with her parents after her relationship with them was destroyed by their divorce years ago. I was glad Elsie was taking a step toward healing, but a part of me was sad that it meant I'd be alone as a result.

I would've spent Christmas with Emma and Aunt Maggie, but Emma had said that she was going to surprise my aunt with a trip to the big city since her mom was gaining her strength back after her battle with cancer. I thought about asking to tag along, but it was hard for Emma to be away from Maggie while she was at college, and I wanted them to have the time together they needed.

Even if that meant I would be alone once again.

The thought had a hollow ache settling into my stomach.

As much as I wanted to take care of myself and not need anyone to help me get by…

I despised being alone.

After letting myself wallow for a while, I got up and flipped through the small stack of mail on my counter. I was terrible at opening my mail and let it build up for a couple weeks until I was forced to go through it. Most of it was junk anyway. Endless credit card offers, utility maintenance coupons—which were hilarious since I lived in an apartment and didn't need them—and countless *Meridel Post* newspapers. I had made it all the way to the bottom, the rest of the stack tossed in the recycling bin, when there was a knock at my door.

The one person who had a key to the building and thus access to my door was—

"Who's your bestest best friend in the whole world?" A muffled voice sang through the wood door.

"Hmm, I think I need to think about it," I answered as I opened it to find my best friend, Elsie. She had a sneaky grin on her face, her dark blonde hair pulled up into a messy ponytail. She wasted no time sauntering in and plopping down on my couch.

"No Jameson tonight?"

Elsie shook her head. "He had his clinic's Christmas

party tonight."

"You didn't go with him?"

Her shoulders shook in a fake shudder. "I think I'd rather poke myself in the eye with a fork."

"What lovely imagery."

Elsie's light laugh filled the room before she patted the couch next to her. "I will accept your gratitude in the form of donuts or chocolate."

I narrowed my eyes as I plopped down next to her. "My gratitude for what?"

Elsie rummaged in her pocket and pulled out a folded piece of paper, flattening it out over her knee before she handed it to me with a smug smile.

It was an advertisement for the *Rising Star Photography Contest*.

Hope wormed its way into my heart as I read the description.

"Where did you get this?" I whispered, holding it up to the light as if I had missed some crucial piece of information.

"Jameson is subscribed to the *Iowa Artist Gazette*, and the flyer was inside the magazine." She grabbed my hand. "The contest is based in England, but it's open to international entrants, and it's specifically for up-and-coming photographers. There's prize money and the possibility of a contract with big photography agencies. This is your second chance, Maya."

I slumped over on the couch, and a groan escaped

my lips. "Maybe I'm not cut out for photography, Els."

"Don't be ridiculous," she scoffed. "You gave me tough love with Jameson last year, and now I'm going to do the same. Your photos are amazing, and you know there's nothing that makes you happier than when you're taking pictures.

"The camera was made for you. I don't know why Oliver won instead of you, but it doesn't matter. You're being given a second chance *now*. Besides, even if it doesn't work out, it won't be the last opportunity. You were made for this, Maya. Don't let your past keep you from living your dreams."

"Being broke sure makes living out dreams hard," I muttered under my breath.

"I heard that." She scowled at me. "Did you even see the prize money?"

With a sigh, my eyes zeroed in on the massive amount listed on the flyer. I Googled how much it was in US dollars and almost fell off the couch. It was equivalent to ten thousand dollars!

My heart pounded in my chest and for a second, I wondered if I was having a heart attack. Or was a racing heart, sweaty palms, and erratic breathing normal? On second thought, maybe it was just a panic attack.

That money would pay off my debt and maybe even get Sunflower Fields off the ground.

"I did you a favor and scoured their website too. Second and third place also win a smaller amount of money. Even if you don't win first place, you could still earn a little cash." Elsie studied me. "I know you're stressed about money."

She was the only person who knew how in debt I was, and how much that prize would mean to me.

This was huge. This could be everything I'd been needing.

And yet...part of me still hesitated. It was a contest in England. What if Oliver entered too? He had to know about it already. What if he won *again?*

I couldn't handle losing to him for a second time.

But I knew I'd regret it if I didn't try.

I flung an arm over my eyes in my usual dramatic fashion and said, "I'll think about it."

Elsie just laughed, knowing that's all the commitment she'd get out of me. "I'll take that donut or chocolate now."

I pried myself from the couch cushions and went to raid my kitchen.

"Oh, just so you know, Jameson and I are planning a Friendsmas in a couple weeks so we can still celebrate with you before we head out of town," Elsie said, and I paused my treat hunting.

"What the heck is Friendsmas?"

"Christmas with friends, silly. We'll make dinner and open presents and be together." She paused, her eyes softening. "I'm sorry we won't be here to spend Christmas with you this year. I could—"

"Nope," I interrupted. "You're not getting out of

reconnecting with your parents. I'll be fine, Els. You enjoy Christmas with Jameson and your family, and I'll enjoy some peace and quiet by myself." I ignored the pang in my stomach, and the bitter taste on my tongue as the words came out.

A thick, heavy silence settled, and I looked over my shoulder to find Elsie wringing her hands in her lap.

"Have you heard from your mom at all?" she finally asked.

At the mere mention of my mom, my muscles twisted into knots.

"You know I don't talk to her. It's been years."

"Maybe—"

"No, Els. We're not going there. She made her choice. It's just how it is."

Elsie was quiet after that, knowing better than to push me where my mother was concerned.

I managed to find a half-empty bag of chocolate chips hiding in the back of my pantry. We left the sad topics behind us while we devoured them, and talked about how things were going with her book deal—her first romantic comedy was set to release in the spring—before we settled in for a night of Hallmark Christmas movies, though we only made it through one before Elsie yawned and pried herself from my couch.

"We're not as young as we used to be," she said through another yawn as she got up and gave me a hug before slipping into her coat and boots. Before Elsie left, she gave me a stern look and said, "Don't forget to enter the contest, Maya," then wished me goodnight.

Once she was gone, I tiptoed back to the couch, eyeing the competition flier as if the paper would grow giant teeth and eat me. My fingers trembled as I picked it up and scanned it for the tenth time. At the bottom was the deadline to enter in big red letters. December thirty-first—the end of the month.

Was Elsie right? Was this my second chance? Maybe Oliver had ruined the first one at Meridel Community College, but did I dare put my heart, not to mention my future, on the line again? If I was smart, I would leave my camera in a bag buried in my closet and never look back, finding something else to fill my bank account.

But...making smart decisions had never been my strong suit. I was too impulsive. That was one reason I was in debt to begin with.

I blew out a long breath, set down the flyer, grabbed the remote, and turned on another Christmas movie. I hated this time of year, but there was something about these cheesy romances that set my aching heart at ease.

For tonight, I would lose myself in someone else's love life, and worry about the photography competition tomorrow.

Oliver

If I thought the racing heart from the coffee was unpleasant, it had nothing on the prickling feeling that was threatening to burst from my skin as I sat in my Jeep outside the auto body shop, preparing to face Maya for the first time in months, praying she wouldn't punch me in the face for all the trouble I had caused.

Whenever I angered her, there was a distinct flash of her blue eyes that gave away that she wanted to punch me. It was either that or she wanted to kiss me, but that might have been wishful thinking on my part.

She probably meant for those looks to scare me away, but I found them strangely endearing.

Should I be concerned that I inspired the girl I liked to violence? Probably.

One time in class she had been fidgeting with a tripod, trying to get the legs to extend. I walked over and tried to take it from her to help her, but instead she got angry, gripped the thing tighter, and yanked it from my hands, simultaneously hitting me in the stomach with the end of it.

She had been far too happy at my grunt of pain, and then barked, "I've got it," and stalked to another table, away from me, and proceeded to ignore me.

Somehow the whole interaction made me like her even more.

Maya was feisty.

I loved it.

My fingers twitched against the button to unbuckle the seat belt, but I couldn't bring myself to push it as I stared at the building in front of me.

The place desperately needed a facelift. What used to be white stucco was now a discolored brownish white, the front door creaked something awful whenever it opened, and the lit sign above the door no longer had every letter of Meridel Auto shining through the snow. Instead, it read "Meri Ato," which was kind of ironic since there was nothing "merry" about the look of the shop.

Being the only auto shop around, I would have expected the owner to put in more work to make the place visually appealing, but then again, in a small town, maybe he just didn't care all that much.

I brought my attention back to the door, still fidgeting

with the seatbelt. Why was I so nervous to see Maya again? Why was her potential reaction to seeing me so frightening?

She already hated me. It couldn't get worse than that.

My phone buzzed in the cupholder, and I flinched. I half expected it to be Maya, letting me know she was here, even though she went inside a few minutes ago. Like the coward I was, I had slumped down in my seat to hide from her as she passed by. It was a moment I was not proud of.

I picked up my phone, but instead of Maya's name, the screen flashed *Dad*.

Great. What does he want now?

I swiped open the message.

DAD

Are you coming to Christmas dinner at your mother's?

I rolled my eyes.

This was another question I had been avoiding for weeks. My mum lived here half the year, not far from Meridel. Her family was from Iowa, and it was hard for her to be in England away from them all the time, so a few years ago she decided to live in the States for part of the year. The time my parents spent apart weakened their relationship, and now he only cared if I was at dinner so that I could be a buffer between them.

Once again, using me.

I was sick and tired of being used.

I sighed, clicking the screen off. My dad had already waited this long for a response. What was a little bit longer? I had finished editing those photos and was on my official break now. I didn't owe my dad anything else.

I took a bolstering breath and forced my limbs to climb out of the car. I ran a hand down my coat to smooth it out before doing the same with my hair and the short beard on my face.

My heart was like a stampede in my chest as I headed inside to face Maya Beck.

Well. Here goes nothing.

5

Maya

"Hey, Paul. Did ya miss me?" I bounced up to the counter with a bright smile on my face, resting my elbows on it like we were old friends.

Paul's head snapped up, and a deep scowl marred his lips when his eyes connected with mine.

"Oh great. You've returned," he deadpanned. "To what do I owe this displeasure?"

I arched a brow. "Are you this nice to all your customers, Paul, or do you reserve this pleasant attitude just for me?"

His scowl deepened making him look like the grumpy cat meme. I didn't know it was physically possible for lips to turn down that far.

Instead of responding to my goading, he just blinked at me, waiting for an answer.

"Oh, is that morse code?" I asked, pointing at his blinking eyes. "Are you trying to tell me something?" Leaning closer, I whispered, "Are you in trouble, Paul? Do you need me to get you out of here?"

Paul's eyes fluttered close with a groan, and he rubbed at his temples. I dropped my fake smile and gave him a scowl of my own.

"Look, Paul. Someone is meeting me here to pay for the car scratch."

"Oh goody." He rolled his eyes and went back to his computer. When I didn't move from my spot at the counter he added, "Why don't you go wait somewhere else until they show up then. Anywhere but next to me."

I tried to give a flirty growl-purr thing, but I had a feeling it sounded more like I was choking on the words instead of being flirtatious. "I bet you just have the ladies all over you with that lovely disposition."

Paul ignored my jab and kept working. I gave an unattractive snort before adjusting my purse to go sit in the chairs along the wall, checking my watch while I walked. I was a few minutes early. I took a seat in the gross plastic chair next to the door. I wanted to see who the car scratcher was before they saw me.

And yes, I realized how stupid that was.

Something about seeing them first eased a bit of anxiety over this meeting.

My palms were cold and clammy, and I rubbed them against my jeans, trying in vain to dry them in case I needed to shake the stranger's hand for some reason. There was nothing worse than a wet handshake. A squeezing feeling constricted my chest making it difficult to breathe.

I didn't know why I was anxious. The person—whoever they may be—was coming to fork over two grand and then they would leave, and this would all be over. I'd get my car fixed and be on my merry way.

Nothing anxiety inducing about that. Right?

Too bad my body hadn't gotten the memo yet.

I pulled out my phone and opened the Sunflower Fields email inbox, praying that there would magically be more photography inquiries that would bring in more money, so I didn't have to work as many hours at Dina's, but of course my inbox still had a big red zero over it, stabbing my dream in the heart for the umpteenth time.

My mind swirled in self-pity, distracting me so thoroughly that when the door to the shop opened and closed, I didn't even pay any attention to the man who walked in.

At least until I heard his voice.

"Hey, mate. I'm supposed to pay for some damage to a car."

My heart went ballistic, ratcheting to an unhealthy pace, my pulse thudding against my eardrums.

No. No no no no.

I knew that voice, that accent, far too well.

"You've got to be kidding me," I exclaimed aloud, though I hadn't meant to.

The guy spun on his heel, eyes wide for a moment

before he shoved his hands in his pockets and gave me a smirk. "Oh, Maya. Hi."

Oliver Lewis stood there, looking his usual smug self, with those black-frame glasses and stubble on his face that was somewhere between a five o'clock shadow and a full beard. The coat he wore screamed "I'm made of money" which made me want to pull all the metal buttons off it.

Of course, it was Oliver. Because why not? That was par for the course of my life. Why did I ever expect anything less? I should have listened to my gut and figured out how to pay for it myself.

"It was *you?*" I snapped, stomping up to him until there were inches between us. His sweet and smoky scent wafted into my nose, bringing back the memory of falling into his arms on the last day of photography class. Phantom hands grabbed my waist, and my ears grew hot. I swallowed and took a step back.

To my surprise, a pink tint colored Oliver's cheeks. He opened his mouth to speak but I cut him off.

"Did you scratch my car on purpose?"

Oliver blinked at me. "You think I would do that?"

"It wouldn't surprise me."

"Why's that, Maya?"

A sliver of my resolve crumbled when he said my name. *Dang you, you blasted Brit and that infernal accent.*

"Because you like to ruin my life, so why wouldn't you scratch my car too?"

His eyes went wide, his mouth gaping as if he were surprised. "I didn't ruin your life."

"You certainly did."

Oliver's eyes softened. "Maya—"

"If you two quarreling lovebirds are about finished, can we get to the part of paying for the car so you both can get the heck out of my shop?" Paul interrupted in an annoying droning voice.

"We're not lovebirds," I snapped at the same time Oliver said, "We're finished."

Why didn't he deny the lovebirds thing?

"No, we're not finished," I bit out, grabbing Oliver's arm, ignoring the jolt that went up my own in the process. "Excuse us for a minute, Paul." I dragged my archnemesis over to the corner then crossed my arms.

"You're not paying for my car, Oliver."

His brows lowered. "I thought you wanted me to. Isn't that why you texted me?"

I shook my head so hard it gave me a headache. "I don't want anything from *you*, least of all your money."

I didn't want to feel indebted to him, and I didn't want to be at his mercy or feel like I owed him something. Which I understood was ridiculous since the damage was his fault anyway. But still.

His shoulders slumped ever so slightly. "Maya..." He sighed, running a hand through his perfectly styled hair. "Just let me pay for the repairs and we can both get on with our lives."

I hesitated for a split second. I couldn't afford to fix the scratch myself. Would it be so bad to let him pay for it?

After another moment, I sighed. "Fine. But I don't like you," I bit out between clenched teeth, making sure he understood that accepting his money didn't mean I wanted to be friends. Of course, I didn't know if he'd even think that in the first place, but my brain was in overdrive, overthinking every part of this.

Oliver stared at me for a long moment, his blue eyes flickering with some emotion I couldn't quite place. "Good. The feeling is mutual." Then he marched back to the counter, leaving me gaping after him.

The mouse of Paul's computer clacked obnoxiously. "All right. For the scratch on the Honda Accord, it'll be two thousand dollars and seventy-three cents."

I cringed at the total, expecting Oliver to be shocked as well, maybe even argue about it, but he handed over his credit card without a word. I squeezed next to him.

"Wait a sec, you're not even going to fight him on the cost?"

Oliver glanced at me before looking back at Paul. "I assumed you already did, which is why you contacted me in the first place." He gave me a slow once-over. "There's no point in arguing. Paul doesn't seem the type to bend to begging either."

Paul continued fiddling with the card reader, ignoring us.

"Two thousand is a lot of money," I retorted. *Thank*

you, Captain Obvious.

The corners of Oliver's mouth twitched. "It is."

"And you're just going to pay it?"

This time he turned to face me. "Yes, Maya. I didn't scratch your car on purpose but that doesn't mean I'm not going to be a gentleman and pay for the damage I caused. I don't expect you to pay for something that wasn't your fault."

Paul handed Oliver his card back and then slid a receipt across the counter.

I wanted to ask Oliver why he was being so nice when all he'd ever done was tease me, but I didn't get the chance.

"I can start your car today, but it won't be ready until after Christmas," Paul said, pulling the metaphorical rug from under my feet.

After Christmas? I tried to stay calm, pushing down the panic that was rising to the surface. "T-that's okay. I'm sure you have a rental car for me to use." When he said nothing, I added, "Right?"

Paul blinked at me, the movement of his eyelids slow and exaggerated. "We're out of rentals."

"What?"

"It's Christmas time. Everyone needs rentals while their cars are in the shop."

"And so do I! How am I supposed to get to work without a car?"

Paul shrugged. "Not my problem."

I let out an angry huff, my hands flexing into fists, about to lunge over the counter and punch Paul in the face when familiar hands—that really shouldn't have been familiar at all—settled on my shoulders and pulled me backward toward the door.

Oliver took the keys from my hand and tossed them at Paul.

"Thank you for your time, Paul. Please let Maya know the moment her car is ready."

The shop owner just waved a hand in dismissal, not bothering to say another word as Oliver dragged me out of the building. I wriggled out of his grasp as we stopped next to a silver Jeep.

"Just what do you think you're doing?" I demanded. "I need a car, Oliver. I need to be able to get to work and it's too gosh dang cold to walk from my apartment to Dina's." I didn't miss his smirk at my avoidance of using real swear words.

I made to stalk back inside and demand that Paul find me a car when Oliver's arms snaked around my waist, pulling my back against his chest. A flood of his scent smothered me, and my muscles relaxed against my will even though I was being held captive by my archnemesis.

"I don't think going back in there is a good idea, Maya." His voice was low in my ear, sending a shiver through me.

"And why's that?" I spat, my breath pooling in the cold air.

"Because you and I both know that you'll probably end up assaulting Paul, and then you'll spend Christmas behind bars. I don't think you want that."

"Did you just accuse me of being violent?"

"I wouldn't dream of calling you *violent*, Maya," he crooned in that magnificent accent of his. "But I *would* call you feisty."

I barked an unamused laugh, and he loosened his hold on me so I could pull away to face him. His blue eyes flickered with amusement.

I fought the urge to stomp my foot like a kid throwing a temper tantrum. "I still need a car, Oliver. I can't wait until after Christmas to be able to get around." My throat constricted, my eyes burning, and I bit my lip to keep it all away. I would *not* cry in front of this man.

"You have a car," he replied, adjusting his glasses on his nose.

At that moment, Paul came outside and glared at me before climbing into my beat-up Accord and pulled it around to the back of the shop.

I gestured at the now empty parking spot. "What car?"

He mimicked my gesture, only his arms flung toward his own car. "Mine."

"Excuse me?"

Oliver shrugged. "Seeing as it's my fault your car is in the shop in the first place, it's only fair that I offer to drive you around until the repairs are complete."

I was shaking my head before he even finished his

sentence. "You're not chauffeuring me around."

He cocked his head. "Why not?"

"Are you kidding? First of all, it's almost Christmas and I'm sure you have family events and dates and girlfriends to woo and whatnot. Second, we hate each other."

Oliver took a step closer, invading my personal space once again, ducking his head to look me in the eye. "First of all, I only have one Christmas dinner planned, and I can work that out. I also have zero dates, and I certainly don't have a girlfriend."

My stomach fluttered, but I took a deep breath, forcing it away.

"Second of all, I never said I hated you."

Our gazes locked and that swooping in my stomach returned like a battering ram.

Well, now. You're just going to have to knock that off, stomach.

"You said you didn't like me five minutes ago."

Oliver dared another step closer, leaning down to murmur in my ear. "Dislike and hate are two very different things." A smirk lit his face as he pulled back, pushing his glasses up his nose again.

It shouldn't have been so hard to tear my gaze from his. I shook my head and stepped away from him.

"Don't be ridiculous," I said, voice quiet. "We hated each other from the moment we met."

He arched a brow. "Speak for yourself."

"What's that supposed to mean?"

Oliver's eyes flicked back and forth between mine for a moment before he cleared his throat. "It's not important. Let me drive you home, and you can think on my offer."

Part of me desperately wanted to continue this conversation to find out how he remembered our first meeting. All I remembered was him going out of his way to be a teacher's pet—snagging the assignment I wanted—gloating about it, and then stealing my desk to top it off. He had acted like we were in high school, not well into our twenties in a college photography class.

I shoved the memory away, my body shivering from standing in the cold.

"Don't you have a job or work to do other than drive me around?"

"I'm on a break," he said.

What the heck does that mean?

"Come on, I'll drive you home." He stood next to his car, waiting with far too much patience.

"Fine," I said. I didn't have another option.

Oliver opened the passenger door for me, and I rolled my eyes at him.

"I can open my own door, Oliver."

A smirk was his only response as he offered his hand to help me get into the Jeep. I ignored it and hoisted myself up and into the seat. He huffed a breath before jogging around the car and jumping in himself. Oliver flicked a ridiculous number of switches before pulling out of the parking lot, and it was a moment later that I realized he had turned on the seat warmer for me.

I blew out a frustrated breath. Not only was I without my own car for the next three weeks, but now Oliver, my own personal Lex Luthor, would be driving me to and from work if I didn't find someone else to give me rides, forcing me to be in his presence?

On top of spending Christmas alone...

I suppressed a sigh. *Merry Christmas to me.*

6

Oliver

An awkward silence filled my Jeep as we drove down the streets of Meridel.

Maya sat curled in on herself in the seat, one elbow propping her chin up on the window. Her entire body was pointed toward the door, making it clear that she didn't want to be here with me, and she *definitely* didn't want to talk.

My throat itched with words unsaid, begging to be blurted out. I wanted to know everything about Maya. Why she was so angry at me for winning that competition, why she thought I ruined her life, what went through her mind when she was taking pictures that made her look so...*alive,* and what would put a smile on that beautiful face of hers. I wanted to know what her laugh sounded like, or what her lips—

No. Stop thinking like that.

I shook my head, trying to expel the thoughts. As much as I desired to learn everything there was about Maya Beck, she had made it clear she didn't want me around. I wouldn't disrespect her wishes…even if I wanted to get closer.

Get a grip, Oliver. Never going to happen.

"Shouldn't you be keeping your eyes on the road instead of on me?" Maya asked, breaking the silence, lifting a brow as she met my gaze. "Or are you looking to damage your car as well?"

My hands tightened on the steering wheel. "I guess you'll never know."

She scoffed. "Are you going to tell me why you hurt Betsy?"

"Betsy?"

"My car, Oliver. Betsy is my car."

My body stilled at the sound of my name in her voice, and I forced a light laugh between my lips. "You named your car *Betsy*?"

Her scowl could have stopped my heart in my chest. "She's old and faithful, and you took her away from me." Maya crossed her arms over her chest.

"Why didn't you name her Old Faithful then?"

Maya snorted, turning her head away from me, probably so I wouldn't see the smile twitching at her lips.

"You didn't answer my question," she replied after

she had stifled her laugh.

"You wouldn't be satisfied with me saying it was an accident and paying for it?"

Maya looked me dead in the eye. "No."

I scrubbed a hand across my face. "It's embarrassing."

A devious light filled her eyes. "Now you *must* tell me."

I adjusted my grip on the steering wheel, trying not to cringe. She'd never let me live this down.

"I...saw you in that field taking pictures. I pulled over and parked next to your car, thinking I would say hi since I was back in Meridel and hadn't seen you since—" I cut myself off, realizing she probably didn't want to be reminded of that day. "Anyway, I was going to say hello, but realized that was probably weird and decided to leave instead."

Something flashed in her blue eyes but I wasn't sure what it was.

"When I turned to go, I slipped on a patch of ice and your car caught my fall. The metal button on my coat got stuck between me and the door and...well you saw the result." I winced. "It truly was an accident."

"Why on earth would you stop to say hi to me?" she asked, her brows lowered in genuine confusion.

Blast. What do I say to keep her from suspecting my feelings for her?

"I, uh, thought I saw a bug?"

I fought the urge to smack my forehead at such a ridiculous response.

Maya blinked. "You thought you saw a bug...across a field...in the middle of winter."

Since I had already committed to this absurd excuse, I was forced to go with it. "Stranger things have happened. Didn't want you to get attacked by the bug."

It was obvious that she didn't believe a word that came out of my mouth—with the way she cocked an eyebrow and pursed her lips, but she didn't fight back and fell silent instead.

I sighed. Someday I would tell her how I felt—maybe—but for now it was best that she didn't know. What would she think if I said those words, if she knew I fancied her? What would she think if I told her that when I said, "feeling is mutual," I actually meant that I *more* than liked her? Would she never want to see me again? Or would she...return my feelings? Maybe even give me a chance?

No, Maya had made it clear that she wanted nothing to do with me. She'd never return my feelings.

Maya twiddled her thumbs in her lap. "So, you're not *purposely* trying to ruin my life then?"

I swallowed my unease and looked at her as I stopped at a stop light. "Is that what you think about me?"

She shrugged. A minute later, I pulled up next to the apartment building she had directed me to. Maya wasted no time throwing herself out of my car, her boots slipping over the ice. I barely managed to skim my fingers across her wrist, trying to stop her before she was out of reach.

"Maya."

She froze, her back to me.

"I swear to you, I never meant to hurt…Betsy. It was never my intention to *ruin your life*. I apologize if I ever made you feel that way."

She looked over her shoulder at me. For a moment, I thought she had taken my apology to heart, her eyes softening, but then they shuttered, and she shook her head.

"Goodbye, Oliver."

Then she slammed the door, leaving me, and the weird fluttering of my heart at our brief touch, behind.

7

Maya

“**P**lease tell me you love me,” I pleaded to Elsie over the phone.

I didn’t even bother eating dinner—not with the knots making a home in my stomach courtesy of Oliver—before plopping face-first onto my bed and calling my best friend.

Elsie’s light laugh filtered through the phone. “That sounds like a trap.” I groaned and she laughed again. “What’s up, Maya?”

My face was still pressed into a pillow, the lavender scent of the calming spray I used on it trying, and failing, to soothe the jagged edges where my anxiety was poking out.

“Oliver is the car scratcher and he hates me and now I have no car so he offered to give me rides and share his car with me!" I whined, but it came out more like, "Oliver...car scratcher...hates me...share his car with me!"

There was a beat of silence before she gasped. "Oliver's the one who scratched your car?"

How she understood any part of my mumbled sentence was a testament to our friendship.

"I told you he hated me, Els." I sighed. "Can you drive me to work for the next couple of weeks?"

An unattractive snort came through the phone.

That's a good sign.

"Back up, start from the beginning," she said instead.

With a sigh, I told her the story of how my archnemesis scratched my car and, even though he'd paid for the damage, I'm now without a car for the foreseeable future.

Elsie was silent for a few moments when I finished.

"Let me get this straight. He made an oopsie, has done everything he can to fix it, even offering to drive you around Meridel, and you still think he hates you."

I scowled, hoping she felt the power of it through the phone. "I think you missed the point."

Elsie retorted, "No, I think *you* did."

"What's that supposed to mean?"

"You've painted this guy to be the devil, but the fact of the matter is, he's doing all the right things. If he hated you, he wouldn't have even left a note on your car. He would've run and never looked back. He's trying to make it right *and* help you. That's not my definition of an enemy."

"Maybe I should get you a new dictionary for Christmas then."

Elsie scoffed. "Maya."

"Elsie."

We both sighed at the same time.

"So, you can't help me out then?" I asked.

"You know I would if I didn't have my book deadline coming up, and we weren't packing and getting ready to go out of town. Jameson is wrapping up things at his clinic so that he can have some time off."

I gave a long, dramatic sigh.

"If Oliver is willing and offering, just take him up on it. It's too cold for you to walk to Dina's and you know it."

"But that means I have to spend more time with him."

I was certain if I had been able to see Elsie, there would have been a sly smile on her face as she said, "Maybe that's not a bad thing."

"I miss the days where you were cynical about men and relationships," I quipped.

"Ha! You have no one to blame but yourself for that change of heart."

I supposed I asked for that. It was thanks to my meddling that my cousin, Jameson, and Elsie had met and fallen in love in the first place.

A dangerous thought crept into my mind. What if Oliver was *my* Jameson?

I quickly shut down *that* train of thought. There was no way.

"What's the worst that could happen, Maya?" Elsie said a moment later. "At the very least, you have a ride to and from work and don't have to be in the cold. And if you're lucky there will be…more."

"I don't need more, Els. I'm fine by myself."

"You can keep telling yourself that, but you know you're just as lonely as I was before you forced me into that photoshoot. I'm not saying you *need* a guy to make you happy, but there's nothing wrong with desiring to have someone by your side, supporting you and loving you. It's hard to put yourself out there, and you know I know that better than anyone, but it's worth the risk, Maya."

Her words had my insides squeezing. I was used to relying on me, myself, and I. I kept telling myself that I was enough and that I was content with that, but Elsie saw through me like no one else. I didn't have to tell her I was lonely. She just knew.

But still. Oliver wasn't the one for me. We barely got along. Elsie had to be wrong. It *wasn't* a good thing for us to spend more time together.

I opened my mouth to argue further, but Elsie interrupted. "I need to go, though. I have to finish this round of edits and do tons of cleaning and packing before Jameson and I head to my parents." Her voice wobbled the tiniest bit at the mention of them.

I imagined it would be hard for her to reconnect with them after being so angry after their sudden divorce, but it would be better for her in the end. Healing was hard, but it would make her stronger.

"I'll talk to you later though?"

"Yeah, okay," I whined.

Elsie laughed. "It's all going to work out, Maya. It's Christmastime, after all." I imagined her wiggling her hands in the air as she gave her best attempt at an operatic voice and sang, "There's magic in the air."

"There's no such thing as Christmas magic, Els."

Her only response was a suspicious giggle as we hung up. I tossed the phone onto the bed and threw an arm over my face. If Elsie and Jameson couldn't help me out, then I would be stuck with Oliver. I had a few other friends, but most of them were far enough from Meridel that it would be a nuisance to ask them for rides.

I opened the calendar app on my phone and counted all the days I'd be forced into Oliver's presence. Thankfully, Dina closed the restaurant the week of Christmas—she liked to take her family on a cruise to get away from the cold for a while—so that eliminated seven whole days that I'd have to be around him.

I smothered my face with my lavender-scented pillow again, praying it would ease the tightness in my stomach.

It didn't.

With a sigh, I resigned myself to texting Oliver and hit send before I could overthink it.

> **ME**
> If the offer still stands, I could use rides to work until my car is fixed.
>
> No one else is available.

Not even thirty seconds passed before my phone buzzed.

OLIVER LEWIS
I'm glad you finally came to your senses.

> **ME**
> This doesn't mean I like you.
>
> You're simply a means to an end.
>
> I'd rather suffer your presence than walk to work in the winter.

OLIVER LEWIS
Glad to know I rank slightly higher than horrendous cold.

> **ME**
> I'd say you're neck and neck.

OLIVER LEWIS
For now. [smiling devil emoji]

I swallowed down the strange flop in my stomach and rolled my eyes.

ME

Pick me up at nine.

After a moment, I added:

ME

Please.

OLIVER LEWIS

Well since you said please.

See you in the morning, Maya.

I clicked the screen off and chucked my phone at the headboard, watching it bounce onto the mound of pillows.

A couple weeks with Oliver Lewis as my chauffeur. That wasn't so bad.

I could do that. Right?

I grabbed my pillow one more time, shoved my face into it, and screamed, just for good measure.

Maya

Oliver was just a little too chipper the next morning as I opened the Jeep door to his smiling face.

"Good morning," he said. I grunted as I crawled inside.

A flood of his cologne smacked me in the face and I was too tired to stop the words from slipping out. "You smell nice."

My body locked up in the middle of putting my seatbelt on. *Why did I say that?*

A too pleased smirk curled his lips, and my cheeks burned. "I mean the *car* smells nice." I tried to correct myself. "Not you."

Oliver huffed a laugh before pulling away from my apartment. "If you say so, Maya."

I gave a dramatic sigh. It was too early for his teasing.

I was not a morning person. It didn't matter what time it was; I simply wasn't made for mornings.

Refusing to risk saying anything else embarrassing, I sipped at the coffee in my hot-pink travel mug, doing my best to ignore Oliver during the ten-minute car ride. I was just starting to doze off again when Oliver's phone rang through the car's Bluetooth, shattering the silence and making me jump.

Oliver glanced at me. "Do you mind if I answer that?"

"It's your car," I replied, turning my gaze to the snow outside.

A moment later a British voice was barking through the speakers. "Are you avoiding me, Oliver? You haven't answered a single one of my messages."

Oliver tensed, his hands strangling the steering wheel. "Sorry, I've been busy."

"Too busy to talk to your father?"

That was Oliver's *dad*? He sounded like a real piece of work. Their conversation hadn't lasted five seconds and *I* didn't even want to talk to the guy.

Oliver's shoulders were up by his ears now. "What do you need?" He glanced over at me, and I averted my gaze, staring at the dashboard, forcing myself to count specks of dust to distract myself.

"Well, firstly, I'm checking that you entered the contest like you said you would."

Out of the corner of my eye, I saw him look at me again.

Contest?

"Not yet."

His father's sigh crackled through the speakers. "The deadline is getting close, Oliver. I'd hate to see you miss out on such an opportunity."

Oliver's jaw twitched. "Isn't it frowned upon, *Dad*, seeing as I'm your son and you're one of the judges?"

His dad scoffed. "Don't be ridiculous. If you're the best photographer, it doesn't matter who your family is."

At the mention of photography, every alarm inside me started going off.

There was no way...he couldn't possibly be talking about the very same contest that Elsie wanted me to enter...right? Surely the universe wasn't *that* cruel to pit me against Oliver Lewis *again*.

I had to be sure, so I pulled my phone out and started Googling, tuning out their conversation. My stomach dropped to my feet when I came across the list of judges for the *Rising Star Photography Contest*. I wasn't sure what Oliver's dad's name was, but there was someone named Leander Lewis, and that was too big of a coincidence to ignore.

Great. Wonderful. I pinched the bridge of my nose. I thought I had a decent chance at winning a prize in the contest, but against Oliver?

All my confidence evaporated at the thought of competing against him once again. And with his dad as one of the judges...did that mean my chances went from slim to none?

Could this get any worse?

"Do it tonight," his dad ordered, breaking me out of my thoughts. "You've wasted enough time already."

Oliver's teeth were likely screaming from how hard he was clenching his jaw.

"Lastly, I need to know if you're coming to Christmas dinner, Oliver."

"I'm always there, aren't I?"

A heavy sigh crackled. "Alone, I presume?"

I risked a glance at Oliver. Every inch of his body was coiled tight like a snake, and his chest rose and fell in too quick a cadence. Why was his dad being such a turd? Was this how he always was?

For a moment, I allowed myself to feel sorry for Oliver. No one deserved to be treated poorly by their parents.

Oliver's hesitation was a second too long, and his dad's disappointed sigh filled the car again.

Then the most idiotic, meddlesome idea I'd ever had popped into my brain, and it prompted me to shout, "Actually, he's bringing me!"

Oliver's head snapped to the side, pinning me with wide, horror-filled eyes.

"Who's that, Oliver?" his father demanded.

"I'm Maya," I answered in a bright, cheery voice when Oliver's mouth continued to open and close like a fish gasping for water. "Oliver's girlfriend."

In the span of half a second, I had concocted a scheme

that would get me close to Oliver's dad and gain me an upper hand in the contest—or at least a fighting chance among all the other entrants.

The only problem was I would have to be around Oliver a *lot* more. My stomach churned at the thought. But surely it wouldn't be so bad. It was a necessary evil—being around my enemy to increase my chances of bettering my future.

It was a necessary—and worthwhile—sacrifice.

My spinning thoughts forced the words to spill out of my mouth before I could think them through. And yes, I realized that might make me a terrible person, but I was starting to feel desperate.

And, though I didn't like to admit it, I hated both the slimy, arrogant sound of his dad's voice, and the cruel way he spoke to Oliver. I may not like the man in the car next to me, but that didn't mean that I wanted him treated badly, especially by his family.

So, as usual, my big mouth got me in trouble, and now I wasn't just a date but Oliver Lewis's fake girlfriend.

Way to go, Maya.

Oliver's eyes threatened to pop right out of his face.

"Excuse me?" his dad sputtered out. "What do you mean *girlfriend*?"

"Just go with it," I whispered, waving frantically at nothing.

"Um...Maya's my girlfriend," Oliver said. "I was going to introduce her at Christmas dinner."

"Oh?" His father sounded skeptical, and it made my muscles twist into knots. "And why have you never mentioned this girl before?"

"I've mentioned her to Mum," Oliver muttered, and it was my turn to gape at him.

Why on earth would he have told his mom about me?

"I need to go, Dad. I'll see you at Christmas dinner."

His father swore but Oliver disconnected the call and cut him off.

Oliver was white as a ghost as he pulled over to the side of the road even though we hadn't made it to Dina's yet. His fingers tangled in his dark hair as his head landed on the steering wheel, shoulders rising and falling in tempo with his erratic breathing.

I was used to seeing Oliver put together and composed, but now he was unraveling. I didn't want to admit it, but I hated the sight of it and found myself wanting to help.

"He sounds like a real winner," I remarked, trying to distract him.

He turned his head to look at me, and I swallowed hard at the pain in his eyes. "Why did you do that, Maya?"

I hesitated for a moment, unsure what to say. It wasn't like I could be honest and tell him I was going to use him to get to his dad. And I certainly couldn't tell him that I felt bad for him because he'd never let me live it down.

"You seemed like you were floundering a little bit

and…your dad was being a jerk. I…wanted to help."

"You wanted to help so you told him you were my girlfriend," he deadpanned.

I winced. "My impulsive ideas aren't always the best."

"Did you consider that it will be obvious I'm lying when I show up to Christmas dinner *without* a girlfriend?"

The anxiety in his voice prompted me to say, "What if it wasn't a lie?"

"Excuse me?"

"Or at least it didn't *look* like a lie," I amended. My ears grew hot from the way his eyes scoured my face.

"I don't think I'm following, Maya."

A frustrated breath slipped through my lips. "I will come to your Christmas dinner with you and *pretend* to be your girlfriend."

Oliver's mouth popped open in an O of surprise.

"Why would you do that?"

Why indeed.

How was I supposed to pretend to like a guy that I hated; who annoyed me to no end and kept screwing up my life?

Maybe that was a bit dramatic, but drama ran in my blood. The truth still remained: he won that spread in the *Iowa Artist Gazette*, ruining the quickest chance to make something of my life. And, if I was honest, him winning instead of me had shaken my confidence so much that I couldn't find the motivation to try harder, or find another way to bring in business.

Because of him, it all felt like a lost cause.

And yet I still offered to help him. I wasn't sure I was ready to examine why.

"You're helping me by driving me to and from work, so let me help by pretending we're dating." I tucked my hair behind an ear, hoping he missed the nervous shake of my hand. "If you want me to, that is."

He studied me for another moment, and I was vaguely aware that we were still sitting on the side of the road and not at Dina's where my shift started soon.

"Let me get this straight. You, Maya, the girl who despises me, wants to pretend to be my girlfriend for Christmas?"

My nose scrunched. "Wow, thanks for making me sound like a psycho."

He ignored my words, still studying my face.

I fixed my eyes on the road ahead of us, unwilling to meet his gaze as I struggled to find a reason he'd accept. "No one should be treated that way—least of all by a parent. Your dad seems like the kind of guy who could use a kick in the butt, and if pretending to be your girlfriend accomplishes that, then I'm willing to do it."

I still felt his gaze on my face and decided to share a truth I knew he'd believe.

"And..." I sighed, unsure why I was admitting this to him. "I don't want to be alone for Christmas."

His eyes softened. "You were going to be alone?"

I nodded, wishing I hadn't brought it up. Oliver

didn't need to know I spent holidays alone. "Usually, I spend it with my cousins and their mom, but Jameson is going out of town with his fiancée this year, and Emma is at college and is bringing my aunt for a visit, so I'll be on my own."

"What about your parents?" I must have made a face because he added, "I'm sorry, I didn't mean to pry."

I wanted to snap at him that it was none of his business, but the reminder of how hard every Christmas was took all the bite out of me. "All you need to know is that neither of my parents are in the picture anymore. I've spent most holidays by myself for years."

His blue eyes somehow softened even more. "I'm sorry."

My eyes burned, but I bit my lip and sniffled to keep the tears away. "Anyway, if you'd like me to pretend to be your girlfriend, I'll do it." I paused before tacking on, "But it doesn't mean I suddenly like you."

Oliver huffed a breath but pulled back onto the road without another word, and a few moments later we were parked in front of Dina's.

"Okay, Maya. You can be my fake girlfriend for Christmas," he agreed and held his hand out for me to shake.

I stared at it, wondering if this was going to be a colossal mistake, and then slipped mine into his.

"It's a deal, Oliver Lewis. Just remember that I secretly hate you."

A lazy grin spread across his face. "For now, Maya. For now."

9

Maya

Dina's was so busy that the hours passed in a daze of fried food and the steady stream of sweat trickling down my spine. By the time my shift was over, and Oliver had dropped me off at home—thankfully without further "Big Mouth Maya" incidents—I felt like I was going to explode. I didn't bother to take my coat off before running across my apartment, socks skidding over the wood floor.

If I was going to be Oliver's girlfriend, then that meant I needed to enter *Rising Star*. I had been on the fence about it up until that fateful phone call in his Jeep, but now I was all in.

The citrus air freshener in my bedroom soothed my anxiety as I searched for that binder of photos. My portfolio was hiding somewhere in my closet and hadn't seen the light of day since Oliver Lewis stomped on my dreams.

My closet floor was a mess and I had to dig deep into a pile of clothes, all the way to the back, tossing everything back into the room from whence it came before I found the binder at the bottom of a stack of college books.

"Ah ha!" I exclaimed, holding it to the sky like Rafiki did to Simba. Ignoring the mess I made, I crawled out of the closet and pulled myself onto the bed, sitting cross-legged. A shaky breath worked itself out of my lungs. I didn't know why I was nervous. I had gone through the portfolio hundreds of times. It *almost* won the Meridel Community College photography competition.

I flipped open the cover. The entirety of the binder contained photographs in chronological order from the start of the class to the end of it. The first pictures were fine, but my skill improved with each page I turned, until I came upon my pride and joy: *The Heart Shot* shoot.

I had begged Elsie and Jameson, who had never met before, to agree to a couples photoshoot where they had to pretend to be in love with each other. It was the coolest idea I had ever had, and it had gained enough traffic through social media that, for a short time, I had enough photography gigs to float by. But far too quickly, they stopped, the money ran out, and now I was stuck at Dina's serving food and coffee.

I scanned through the photos, marveling at how beautiful they turned out. The lighting in that sunflower field had been absolute perfection, and Elsie and Jameson had had instant chemistry.

Plopping onto my back, I stared at the ceiling. *The Heart Shot* pictures were great, but could they win an international competition? Or would I just set myself up to be disappointed and broken once again?

I chose not to see the fact that it was based in England, the same place Oliver Lewis was from, as an ill omen, even with his dad pushing for him to enter as well.

What was the harm in submitting my photos? As crushing as it would be not to win, regret would be a two-ton monster sitting on my shoulders for the rest of my life, whispering in my ear all the horrifying what-ifs that might have happened if I didn't enter.

Besides, not only would it be amazing exposure if I won, but that prize money would pay off all my debt. I could move forward with my life goals, save up to buy my own place, and bury that dark part of my past for good. I'd be able to take pictures because I loved it, because it brought me joy, not because I was worrying about how to pay my bills or put food in my stomach.

Just the thought of being debt-free was enough for me to roll off the bed, run back into the living room, and pull out my laptop. In a few clicks, I entered all my information into their website, including the pictures from Elsie and Jameson's photoshoot.

I blew out a long breath, my finger shaking over the

mouse before I clicked submit.

As if the universe knew that I had taken a big chance yesterday and was determined to make my life miserable as a result, my phone buzzed with a text just as I swiped my timecard to leave work the next day.

OLIVER LEWIS

Hey Maya, I'm going to be a few minutes late to pick you up. Sorry! Be there as soon as I can.

My stomach dropped as I read the words. It had been the world's longest shift at Dina's with way more tourists than usual, meaning I didn't have my usual nice Meridel customers. Instead, I was plagued by rude city people that were demanding and cruel.

All I wanted to do was go home, throw on my pajamas, curl up in bed, and watch reruns of *How I Met Your Mother* for the eighteen thousandth time. Maybe stuff my face with some lasagna and brownie batter ice cream. Separately, of course. I'm not *that* weird.

An ill-timed reminder flashed across my phone.

Don't forget to get groceries, girl.

Dang my stupid phone reminders. And dang me for not getting groceries before my car went into the shop. I was pretty sure the only thing in my kitchen right now was a package of ramen and some Kraft Singles. Those things never expired; I was certain of it. Lasagna and ice cream would have to wait.

I chewed on my lip as I considered my options. I wasn't about to ask Oliver to take me to the grocery store, and, unfortunately, Wally's Market hadn't subscribed to the idea of grocery delivery yet, so there would be none of that either.

I loved Meridel, I really did, but sometimes it was too small, too constricting. It was like an old person, full of knowledge and wisdom, yes, but when you handed them new technology, they tried to shove it into their mouth and eat it instead.

Even still, the thought of leaving made my heart ache. This was home.

"Focus, Maya," I said, shaking my head at how I got off track from food options to nostaliga. Since Dina always closed early on Thursdays, getting food here wasn't an option. The kitchen had already shut down.

My stomach gave a fierce growl as I pulled on my coat and headed outside to wait for Oliver. It was a mild December day with temperatures in the forties, which wasn't *terrible* for standing outside, only uncomfortable. My breath clouded in the air in front of me, and I pulled on my gloves to stave off the chill.

Ramen and fake cheese for dinner? My stomach rumbled in protest, and I put a hand against it. "I know, stomach, but I don't have another option right now," I mumbled and fell deeper into self-pity over the pitiful dinner I was about to have.

You could just ask to eat dinner with Oliver.

If I could have slapped my inner voice, I would have done it in a heartbeat. There would be no dinners, no movies, no dates, no spending extra time with him. He was my archnemesis for a reason. I was doing him a favor like he was by driving me around, and that was it. Limited contact only.

My stomach growled again, and I stomped my foot like a child. I was cold, tired, and hungry, and he was very, very late. I dug into my purse, looking for my phone so I could ask where he was when his Jeep pulled up next to the curb.

He threw open the door for me. "Hey, Maya. Sorry I'm late."

I grumbled and climbed into the car. He flipped on the seat warmer for me, but I was too annoyed and cold to be grateful.

Oliver studied my face for a moment before pulling back onto the road.

After another few tense seconds, I demanded, "Why are you late?" It was rude, but hangry Maya had taken over.

Oliver arched a brow at me before turning onto Main Street, then leaned forward to pick up a grocery bag on the floor between us. "I was picking up dinner for you. It wasn't quite ready when I got there so I had to wait."

Regret snapped through me like a slap to the face. "What?"

"I was driving back from the next town over and saw a takeout place. I figured you'd been serving food enough today and wouldn't want to cook. So, I picked up dinner." His expression was so genuine, it stunned me.

Oliver...brought me dinner? "Why would you do that?"

He shrugged, his lips twitching. "It's the least I could do. You're helping me with my dad situation."

Oh. That's right. It was nothing more than a thank you. Why did that leave disappointment settling in my gut like a bad burrito? What did I think it was? My enemy being genuinely nice? Ha. Yeah, right.

"I, um...I'm sorry I snapped at you." I didn't want to thank him, but the smell had filled the car, and my stomach had full control over my mouth at this point.

Oliver smirked at me. "It's all right. You're just hangry."

Why did such a ridiculous word sound beautiful in his accent? A fierce gurgle erupted from my body.

Oliver chuckled. "Let's get you home and some food in your stomach."

Music to my ears.

Oliver

"This bag of food is dangerously heavy, Maya. I think I should carry it for you," I teased, holding the plastic bag above my head and out of her reach.

We had been standing outside her apartment building in a standoff for a solid five minutes. Maya didn't want me to come inside, but she had yet to give me a genuine reason why I shouldn't. I was desperate for any ounce of time I could get with this woman, and I wasn't a quitter.

Even if my excuse of a heavy takeout bag was a little far-fetched and made me look foolish.

Maya arched a brow. "If it's so heavy then how can you hold it over your head?"

"Easy. Under all this," I gestured to my coat, "I'm all muscle."

A blush spread over her cheeks as her gaze slid over me, and it filled me with immense satisfaction. The early morning workouts suddenly felt like the best decision I had ever made. I wasn't a bodybuilder by any means, but I looked good, and I wasn't afraid to admit it.

"Come on, Maya. There's enough for two here, and I don't bite. Let me carry it for you."

Her lips bent into a frown. "I don't need a big muscley man to carry things for me, Oliver."

Some men might have backed down at her words, or perhaps given up, but to me they served as gasoline, fueling my desire to be closer to her. I knew even a small spark would lead to our inevitable burning, resulting in the most exquisite pain I'd ever experienced. Like the sting of linework in a tattoo before the final masterpiece is revealed. But I had to get her to see it.

"Maybe not," I conceded. "But maybe this is more of a want than a need."

"I don't *want* to have dinner with you, either."

A sigh escaped my lips as I lowered the bag to my side. "Humor me, Maya. It's just dinner. Is there something wrong with your apartment? Some secret you don't want me to know?"

Maya rolled her eyes.

"Are you secretly a hoarder? Or maybe you only clean when the moon is full?" She snorted. "Or..."

I lowered my voice to a whisper. "Do you keep dead bodies in your closet?"

Maya's face contorted in outrage before she shoved my shoulder. "If I kept corpses in my apartment, I wouldn't hesitate to bring you upstairs so you could join them."

I cocked my head, taunting her. "Prove it."

Her petite frame trembled in frustration, and I expected her to put her foot down, likely on my toes, and demand I go away. But then she grumbled a curse under her breath before unlocking the door and walking inside the building.

A small smile curved my lips. *Victory.*

Pressing the lock button on my car keys, I followed her. It was a silent elevator ride to the fourth floor, and I fought the urge to nudge Maya's shoulder as we walked down the hall to her apartment. The chair rail along each wall was decorated with Christmas garlands, and the faint scent of stale cigarettes lingered in the air.

At the end of the hall, she paused before apartment 415. "Just...don't judge me, okay?" Her voice was soft, tentative.

"I won't judge you for dead bodies, Maya. Though I might recommend you get some help."

She punched my arm, and I laughed.

I braced myself, preparing for something bad, maybe a messy apartment with clothes everywhere, dishes and trash all over the kitchen, or the pungent odor of a litter box if Maya turned out to be one of those crazy cat ladies.

But instead, it was...spotless.

Not a thing was out of place. There wasn't a single

dish in the kitchen sink, or undergarments lying in the middle of the floor, and definitely no odor. In fact, the gentle scent of citrus essential oil filled the air. I arched a brow as Maya turned to gauge my reaction.

"I'm disappointed, Maya. Not a single whiff of corpses to be found. You worried for nothing." I nudged her shoulder, but she stood stiff as a board.

"I don't like mess," she admitted, her shoulders tensed as she shoved her hands into her pockets. "Clutter and dirt make me anxious."

Understanding flooded through me. Maya struggled with anxiety too? An ache went through my heart at the thought.

"And why would I judge you for that?" I asked.

She shrugged. "Some people find it intimidating, and when you add in the word anxiety on top of it, it's usually *adios buddy*."

I glanced around again, trying to understand why anyone would have a problem with a clean house. It didn't scare me, and neither did her admission to struggling with her mental health.

I smiled. "Well, lucky for you I don't know Spanish. Looks like you're stuck with me."

Maya snorted before covering the sound with a shaking hand, her ears turning red. Unable to help myself, I took hold of her hand, pulling it away from her face, and settled it onto my chest, right over my racing heart. She took a step forward, looking up at me with confused eyes.

"You don't need to worry about me judging you, Maya. I'm not easily scared."

"You say that now, Oliver, but everyone leaves at some point."

I squeezed her hand tighter against my chest, wishing I could force reassurance into her through the contact.

"Who taught you that?" I dared to ask. She was so close now I could smell the faint fruity scent of her perfume.

Her lips parted, an answer waiting on her tongue, but then her eyes shuttered, and she pulled out of my grasp.

Maya shook her head and asked, "Can we eat now?"

I wanted to keep talking, wanted to know whatever she was about to say, but I put my desire aside and headed into the kitchen. "Of course."

The bottle of wine in the bag clinked as I set it on the counter before pulling out a box of pasta, an insulated bag of garlic bread sticks, and a third box of chocolate cake, which I slipped into the fridge when Maya wasn't looking. Her fridge consisted of a half empty carton of milk and a package of cheese slices.

It wasn't my job to protect her or take care of her. And yet...in that moment all I wanted to do was whisk her down the road to Wally's and tell her to fill her cart with anything she wanted. Maya was strong, I didn't doubt that for a second, but maybe she felt the need to portray that she was okay when she really wasn't.

I swallowed down the lump in my throat and pushed away my desire to help for the moment, taking the plates that Maya offered me, and dished out dinner.

"I hope you like Italian," I said, trying to fill the silence that settled between us. Maya was tense, fidgeting with her hands, her eyes darting back and forth between the food, me, and the rest of her apartment.

"Who doesn't?" Maya responded a beat too late, her voice quiet.

Once again, my inner protector wanted to ask what was wrong, but I didn't want to push her too much.

I hoped that at the end of this dating farce that Maya realized I wasn't trying to upheave her life, and maybe she'd end up returning my feelings too. We just had to work through why she hated me so much first.

But I was standing in her apartment—feeding her food. That was a start.

Maya took her plate and led me around the corner to the barstools on the other side of the island. We settled into our seats, and I poured each of us a glass of wine, and she wasted no time digging into her pasta.

"So...did you enter that contest your dad wanted you to enter?" she asked as she twirled a fork through her noodles.

"Unfortunately."

She glanced up at me through her lashes.

"Unfortunately? You mean you didn't want to?"

"Not really, but I have a difficult time telling him

no," I admitted. "He only wants me to enter because it benefits him, but I have no interest in winning something else." I fought a cringe as I glanced at her, hoping she wouldn't take my words as boastful.

"Your dad wouldn't support your decision to not enter?"

I huffed an unamused laugh. "My father is selfish and only thinks of himself."

With that comment, Maya fell quiet.

I thought about telling her more about the photography contest, and suggesting she enter too—she was talented enough to win, I had no doubt—but I didn't want to give my father any fuel against her. He'd see her as a threat to me—and to his own business—and with him as a judge, I didn't know what scheming he'd try to pull.

As we ate in silence, my eyes wandered over Maya's apartment. It was a cute little one bedroom with a small balcony off the living room that overlooked a pond behind the building.

Yet something felt off. It wasn't the cleanliness of the place, or even that everything was shades of white, tan, and gray. No, it was the fact that it was December, and there wasn't a single Christmas decoration in the entire place.

There wasn't a tree in the corner or lights stringing the deck like everyone else's. There wasn't even a Christmas candle filling the air with cinnamon and pine, or a hand towel with Santa's head on it.

I cleared my throat, eyes scanning the place to make

sure I didn't miss anything. "Maya?"

"Hmm?" Her mouth was full of breadstick, and she didn't bother to look at me.

"Why don't you have any Christmas decorations?"

Maya stilled before blinking at me, as if I had spoken a foreign language. She set down the breadstick and wiped her hands and mouth with a napkin.

"I don't do Christmas."

"Do you celebrate a different holiday?"

She shook her head.

"Then what do you mean you don't *do* Christmas?"

She sighed. "I mean, I don't decorate, I don't do presents, and I don't really celebrate it at all."

"Why?"

Maya shrugged. "It's not much fun to celebrate a holiday alone year after year, so I just...stopped celebrating. It's stupid to gift myself presents, and putting up a tree alone isn't enjoyable."

My brows lowered as I watched the way her shoulders slumped, her body curling into itself. She moved her fork in circles, playing with the remnants of her dinner.

I took a chance and asked, "Maya...why do you spend Christmas alone?"

Silence. And then—

"Get out," she said, the suddenness catching me off guard. She stood, grabbed my arm, and led me to the door.

"What?"

"Leave, Oliver. Now."

"Maya—"

"No. You don't get to know these things. You don't get to know my past. We're not friends." We stopped in front of the door, and she gestured for me to leave. "I want you to go."

My stomach sank. Words escaped me as I tried to process how we had gone from a pleasant dinner to her kicking me out. It had been a harmless question. Hadn't it? I replayed it over in my mind and didn't understand why she'd have such a strong reaction.

"Please." Her voice broke, and her eyes glistened.

Instinct had me taking a step toward her, wanting to understand, but Maya stepped back, out of my reach. The food I ate swirled in my stomach at the thought that I had inadvertently hurt her—again.

"All right, Maya. I'll go." I stepped into the hallway.

I turned back, wanting to see her face one more time before I left, and winced as she slammed the door in my face.

Resting my head against the door, I murmured, "There's cake in the fridge."

The sound of her sniffles haunted me the entire walk to my car.

Maya

My dad left when I was a kid, and it taught me something important. And afterward when my mom chose her career over taking care of me, it solidified what I had learned: everyone left eventually. Since no one cared enough to stick around, the only person I could rely on was myself.

And so, ever since then, I held everyone at arm's length, letting them see the big, loud pieces of me, like my lack of a filter or my faked confidence, and keeping the small, tiny things that meant the most to me tucked away. That way, when someone inevitably left, they didn't walk away with all my pieces.

Elsie, Jameson, and Emma were the only people to go against everything I'd ever learned, but Elsie and Jameson were getting married, and they wouldn't be around as much anymore. Elsie would still be my best friend, but I would never be her first choice again. Meanwhile Emma was in the city, chasing her own dreams, and it was difficult for us to stay in touch when she was so busy.

I groaned, shoving the last bite of cake in my mouth, and pushed the plate, and those feelings, away.

I didn't like kicking Oliver out. He had been nothing but nice to me, and yet that question had my insecurities going into a tailspin and all I wanted was for him to leave by *my* choice rather than his.

The question he had asked wasn't the problem. It was the can of worms it opened up.

Namely: I had no one.

The last thing I needed was my archnemesis thinking I was a pathetic, unlovable loner.

But he would see it—eventually. They always did.

That's why the string of dates I had been on in the past year never went further than the first date. I was too scared to let anyone get close enough to see the real me, afraid that once they did, they'd leave for sure. I'd rather quit before feelings could develop. Then I couldn't get hurt when they left.

So, here I sat on my couch, stomach full of pasta and cake, alone.

Just like every night.

The next morning brought a heavy dose of reality mixed with shame.

Oliver Lewis, the man who had teased me and tripped me and made me think I was a rival he hated, was kinder than I ever imagined. I was having a hard time reconciling the two different versions of him. Did he hate me and see me as someone he needed to crush to get ahead or had all the teasing and taunting been a cover-up for something else? I never imagined that Oliver could be nice to me, but being outside of a classroom setting had shown me a side to him I didn't think existed.

I didn't hate it.

And my response to that had been to slam the door in his face. I was still kicking myself over it. It shouldn't have been a big deal for him to ask me about Christmas. I shouldn't have gotten so defensive and upset.

But there was something about him asking me personal questions like that, prying into the aching pieces of me that I kept hidden, that caused me to kick him out.

And even worse, I hated that I felt bad about it—especially when I remembered the way his face fell as I closed the door on him.

Which was why I despised standing on the curb, waiting for him to arrive to drive me to work. This little arrangement was terrible. Not only did I embarrass myself the night before, but now I had to face him the next day. What would I even say to him?

Did I apologize? Did I try to explain why I kicked him out?

Or did I just pretend everything was fine, and that last night had never happened?

I was momentarily saved from making a decision as Oliver's Jeep pulled up next to me, the door popping open a second later.

"Good morning, Maya," Oliver's deep voice was soft as I climbed in, his accent making my heart stutter. The car smelled like his sweet and smoky cologne, and it made me lightheaded—in a good way. His black coat was unbuttoned, revealing a fitted black button-down shirt that left little to the imagination as to the muscle beneath it. Why was he so...buff?

"Morning," I muttered back, unable to meet his gaze.

"Did you have a good evening?"

Oliver's hands clenched the steering wheel, but otherwise his face was relaxed, seemingly unbothered by what happened last night. When he took his eyes off the road to glance at me, I hurried to look away.

"It was fine."

He nodded before turning his attention back to the road, and a tense silence filled the Jeep. I didn't want to bring up last night or talk about why I'd made him leave, so I held my breath, silently hoping he didn't mention it either.

When we were halfway to Dina's, he cleared his throat, his musical accent filling the car.

"Maya, you don't have to explain why what I said was wrong last night, but just know that I will listen if you want to tell me what I did to offend you. I'd like to understand."

For a moment, I gaped at him. Who was this man? Anyone else would have been angry and upset that I slammed the door in their face. But Oliver wanted to... understand?

I scratched my head, needing to do something with my hands. "You didn't do anything wrong, Oliver."

He quirked a brow. "Do you often kick out people for no reason then?"

"It's complicated," I said with a shake of my head. Dina's restaurant appeared down the road. We didn't have enough time for this conversation. I gave him a weak smile, hoping that would keep him from asking more, but the blasted Brit was persistent.

"I can deal with complicated, Maya."

"Are you sure about that?"

"Try me."

In less than thirty seconds we'd be pulling into Dina's parking lot, and the thought of opening up to Oliver, to someone who would leave once he saw how crazy I was, made my heart pound in my chest.

My palms grew clammy, and it was suddenly hard to breathe. I gripped my knees, squeezing my eyes shut, trying to calm the anxiety that had seized my body.

"Maya?" Oliver's voice was far away, at the end of a long tunnel, muffled like he was underwater.

My hands were too hot on my legs, my leggings growing damp from the sweat that had accumulated beneath them. I gasped for air but couldn't find any relief from the squeezing feeling in my chest.

And then warm hands cradled my cheeks, turning my head.

"Hey, breathe." Oliver's blue eyes rimmed in gold came into focus, his brows low in concern.

His thumbs drew soft lines across my face, in time with his calmer breathing, and I latched onto it, forcing my breathing to mimic his. His touch drew out the anxiety. Seconds or minutes later, I wasn't sure, I closed my eyes, drinking precious air into my lungs.

His hands didn't move from my face. I didn't know how long he held me like that, but when my mind finally focused, I realized that we were parked at Dina's. We were so close he was practically sitting in the seat with me.

Oliver was inches away. Now that my anxiety had eased, a strange feeling flickered in my stomach that had me wanting to lean forward into his arms and be held by him.

"Maya?" His voice was soft, breaking me from my traitorous thoughts.

"I'm fine," I whispered, though from the way my voice shook, it was clear I wasn't.

He held onto me for another moment before pulling

his hands away, his fingers dragging across my skin in the most excruciatingly exquisite way. I bit my lip to hold back a whimper.

"Does that happen often?" he asked.

"What?"

"Do you often have panic attacks?"

His face remained blank, void of the judgment I had come to expect. Very few people knew that I struggled with anxiety, and I always hated that they either looked down on me because of it, or gave me eyes full of pity.

I didn't want judgment, and I certainly didn't want pity.

When someone was forced to grow up too soon and learn to take care of themselves alone, there were bound to be mental health effects along the way. I just wished people wouldn't look at me like I was broken, or like something was wrong with me.

But Oliver wasn't looking at me like that. I couldn't quite place the emotion swimming in his eyes.

"I get them too," he admitted.

Understanding. That's what it was.

Shock snapped through me like lightning. Oliver Lewis always appeared so cool, calm, and collected on the outside. I never would have pegged him as someone who struggled with anxiety. Although, most people would have said the same thing about me. Big, loud Maya, remember? Only the big pieces, none of the vulnerable, struggling parts.

"Really?" I asked, looking down at my hands. It wasn't

quite shame flowing through me, but something like it.

A finger touched my chin, lifting it up so I met his gaze.

"Really. I'm sorry you deal with it too."

We were in dangerous territory now. If I didn't get out of this car, I was going to bare my soul to my enemy, and Oliver Lewis would see Maya Beck break down into tears.

I sniffled, blinking against the burning in my eyes. His fingers grabbed my hand as I turned to climb out. I cringed at how sweaty mine were, knowing he must think I was repulsive, but he squeezed harder.

"I know you don't like me, Maya, but I'm here...if you ever need to talk."

The words were like ice numbing a burn, soothing the anxious pit my stomach was. How did this man know exactly what to say? How did he both calm me and make my heart race?

A single tear slipped from my eye, and I cursed beneath my breath.

Oliver swiped his thumb across my cheek, erasing the evidence that I was breaking apart in his presence.

"You don't have to pretend with me, Maya."

And with those words, every wall I had ever built around my heart tripled in size. Cement block after cement block encased all of me. I pulled from his grip and climbed out of his Jeep.

"Pretending is the only way to survive, Oliver."

Oliver

Pretending is the only way to survive.

Maya's words haunted me for the rest of the day. I hated that she felt that way, and that it forced her to keep her walls up around me. I tried to shove the thoughts away, but they kept circling back.

I was grateful for my break from work, and subsequently my father, but I didn't account for the boredom I'd experience not having anything to do. Since I traveled back and forth from England, I didn't have many friends in Meridel.

And, if I was honest, without photography, I wasn't sure who I was or what I was good at. I thought about trying a new hobby, but that didn't feel right either.

Which was why I had nothing better to do than to

sit in Dina's parking lot for the last hour of Maya's shift, waiting to drive her home. My fingers tapped an anxious rhythm against the steering wheel, my eyes glancing at the clock on my dashboard every few minutes, watching it drag toward six o'clock.

Truthfully, I didn't mind acting as Maya's chauffeur. It gave me something to do while I wasn't working, and it let me spend more time with her. The more I saw her, the more desperate I was for her, like a dehydrated person was for water.

A couple minutes before the end of her shift, a car pulled into the spot next to mine. The driver was singing along to muffled rock music emanating through the closed windows. She looked vaguely familiar. Where had I seen her before?

She went inside Dina's and emerged a minute later, arm-in-arm with Maya. Then it hit me. She was the girl from Maya's stranger photoshoot last year.

A memory flashed through my mind of when Maya had presented her photoshoot to the class. Not only were the pictures brilliant and full of life, capturing both the light and landscape, but the absolute joy on her face as she showed off the photos—it had taken my breath away. That was the first moment I knew my crush was more than *just* a crush.

Instead of heading toward my Jeep, Maya didn't even spare me a glance before following her friend. Sudden panic surged in my gut. Had I missed something?

I fished my phone out of my pocket to double check if I had a text from Maya explaining why she wasn't crawling inside my Jeep, filling the car with her fruity perfume that I was becoming addicted to.

The screen on my phone was blank and I made a quick decision to hightail it out of my car.

"Maya," I called, and she froze, her shoulders rising to her ears.

Her friend cocked her head as she looked first at me and then Maya.

"Did you still need a ride?" I asked since she hadn't turned around to face me.

"You know him, Maya?" her friend asked, nodding her head in my direction.

Maya's shoulders slumped as she spun on her heel to look at me, pulling that fake mask on, the one that she wore with everyone else to make them think she was doing great. What would she think if she knew I saw straight through it?

"Oh, hey, Oliver. I, uh, forgot you were picking me up tonight. Elsie and I were going to grab dinner." She hooked a thumb over her shoulder.

Forgot? Right, because that made sense when I was her only means of transportation.

"Oh," I responded, like an idiot, then cleared my throat. Did she hear the disappointment in my voice? "Not a problem." I waved a hand in dismissal and turned to get back in my Jeep. "Have a good time."

"Did you want to join us?" Elsie called, freezing me in my tracks. Maya's trepidation was like needles stabbing at my skin, even from feet away.

"I'm sure he has better things to do, Els," Maya chided.

Her words wiggled under my skin, and a flash of a night without Maya, going home to my empty house *again*, had me opening my mouth.

"Actually, I'd love to."

"You really don't have to—"

"I'd love to," I repeated, holding Maya's gaze.

"Great!" Elsie's voice was vibrant like tinkling bells. "We'll meet you at Get In My Belly."

I nodded, giving Maya a wink that made her cheeks redden before we all got in our cars and left Dina's. Get In My Belly was a local restaurant in the next town over that was somewhere between a bar and fast-food establishment. It was a strange mix of the two—with plenty of greasy food but amazing drinks and appetizers too.

Thirty minutes later, the three of us were seated in a booth, me on one side and Elsie and Maya on the other. Baskets of food were scattered in front of us, and country music blasted through the speakers.

"So, let me get this straight," Elsie said, a waffle fry shoved in her cheek, "you two are going to pretend you're dating at Oliver's family Christmas, but you hate each other?"

Maya said, "Mmhmm," at the same time I said, "I don't hate her."

Elsie cocked her head as she looked between us. Could she see my hidden feelings for Maya?

"Don't you think your family will see right through you guys?" Elsie fixed her brown eyes on me.

"How do you mean?"

She gestured to Maya then to me. "For starters, you're not even acting like a couple. Maya, you should be sitting next to Oliver."

"We're not actually dating, Els," Maya argued.

"But no one's going to believe you if you don't even *act* like you're together. You need to practice." Elsie's leg lifted from beneath the table, her snow boots dripping water onto the seat as she kicked Maya out of the booth. "Go sit by him."

Maya's face twisted in fury. "Els—"

"Go."

I could've scooped Elsie up and given her a giant hug—that's how excited I was that she was forcing Maya into my vicinity so we could practice being a real couple.

I had wanted to suggest it for a while—my dad would be suspicious of us if we didn't act like we were dating—but I didn't know how to bring it up when her walls were already so high. The last thing I wanted was for her to back out, leaving me to face that dinner alone.

With a sigh, Maya scooted into the seat next to me. Her fruity perfume—like pears mixed with some sort of citrus scent—overwhelmed my senses.

"Good," Elsie said. "Now, Oliver, put your arm

around her."

"Elsie," Maya whined, keeping a careful distance between us in the booth.

Elsie simply fixed her with a death glare. "You meddled in my relationship, Maya. Now it's my turn." The two friends glared at each other, and I squirmed in my seat.

"Oliver, arm," Elsie ordered, not breaking eye contact with Maya.

Wasting no time, I put my hand on Maya's waist and scooped her into my side, huffing a laugh when she let out a small yelp, before settling my arm over her shoulder.

"I don't bite," I whispered in her ear, feeling immense satisfaction when she shivered as my lips brushed her skin.

In her typical feisty fashion, she shrugged my arm off her shoulder, but I took advantage of the movement and skimmed my fingers down her arm before wrapping my hand around her waist.

Maya fixed her friend with another glare. "Is this really necessary?"

Elsie smirked. "You could at least try to look like you're enjoying being held by your *boyfriend*."

"I think I liked it better when I was the one giving *you* relationship advice."

Elsie laughed but then her attention snagged on something behind us before another voice joined us.

"Sorry I'm late," a man said, slipping into the booth

next to Elsie. He had dark hair, hazel eyes, and dimples that pierced his cheeks as he smiled at her. He, too, looked familiar. "Got stuck at the clinic."

"That's okay," Elsie said, planting a firm kiss on his lips, and I couldn't help but notice how Maya looked away. "Oliver, this is my fiancé, Jameson."

"Nice to meet you," Jameson said, reaching his hand across the table, shaking mine.

"You too, mate. You're the other half of that photo-shoot Maya did for class, right?"

"Guilty," he said with a smile, pulling Elsie to his side. "Wouldn't be engaged to this one without it."

Their love was tangible, and I wanted to reach out and grab it to take some for myself.

"You invited him?" Maya asked, crossing her arms.

Jameson snorted. "Nice to see you too, cousin."

Maya stuck her tongue out at him, and I chuckled.

Elsie shrugged. "When Oliver joined us, I figured it was no longer a girl's night and invited Jameson. Now it's a double date." She winked, and Jameson planted another kiss on her cheek.

"You could've asked me first," Maya grumbled.

"Go with the flow, Maya," Jameson replied. "Surely dinner with your best friend, cousin, and..." He paused, glancing at me as if unsure what to refer to me as.

"Her boyfriend," Elsie finished, and Jameson's eyes widened. It looked like he might have been sizing me up.

"You actually got Maya to be your girlfriend?" The

shock was clear in his voice.

"I'm not his girlfriend." Maya slumped farther into her seat. I poked her side in a soft rebuttal and didn't miss the way she squirmed. Was she ticklish?

That could be fun.

"For all intents and purposes, until after Christmas, you are. So, start acting like it," Elsie retorted.

They stuck their tongues out at one another, causing Jameson and I to chuckle at their grand display of maturity.

"I think I'm missing something here," Jameson admitted, gesturing between all of us.

Rubbing the back of my neck, I explained, "Maya is pretending to be my girlfriend for my family Christmas dinner in exchange for me being her chauffeur while her car is being repaired."

"You forgot the part where *you* damaged said car," Maya sassed around a bite of burger.

Jameson's eyes flashed with amusement. He cocked his head as he looked at her, narrowing his eyes.

"That's very un-Maya-like of you."

"What are you talking about?"

He gave a shrug. "Fake dating is so against the Maya I know. Your heart is like Jericho, and you keep it that way on purpose. Even if it is fake, there's an opportunity for real feelings to develop, and you avoid *those* like the plague."

His view of Maya intrigued me. It was all things I had suspected or observed about her. Maybe Jameson would fill me in on why Maya kicked me out of her apartment after asking her what I thought was a harmless question.

"You don't know what you're talking about," Maya scoffed, though she blushed.

Jameson opened his mouth to argue, but Elsie put her hand over his.

"Leave her be. She has her reasons, and it's not our place to judge." She turned her brown eyes to her best friend. "But, while I won't judge, I also won't sit back and let you ruin this fake dating thing. I think it will be good for you." Elsie took a sip of her drink. "So, start acting like you're dating."

"Is this how it was when I meddled in your relationship?" Maya asked, glaring daggers at her.

"Yes," Jameson and Elsie answered in unison, without hesitation.

Just as Maya opened her mouth, likely to say something she'd regret, a giant platter of cake smothered in vanilla ice cream was delivered to our table. I had taken a risk, ordering it before we even sat down for dinner, but I wanted to do something nice for Maya, and it was the best I could do with what I had to work with.

The three others looked at it with giant saucer eyes.

"I didn't order that," Elsie breathed.

"Me neither," Maya said.

Jameson wasted no time in picking up a spoon and digging in. I followed suit.

Maya looked at me and I admitted, "My sweet tooth

is gigantic." Then I shoved a huge bite of cake into my mouth, delighted as she watched every second of it. I might have exaggerated dragging my lips over the spoon to drive her crazy.

Would that even drive her crazy?

Or was Maya unaffected by my attempts at wooing her?

Wooing her? What is wrong with me?

"Thanks, man," Jameson said through a mouthful of ice cream, fist bumping me across the table.

"No worries, mate."

"Mate," Jameson repeated before shoving another bite in his mouth. "How long have you been in America?"

I swallowed down a big bite of cake before answering. "I lived here for about six months a year and a half ago. That's when I met Maya in our photography class. I went back to London for a year to finish up some work projects, but I'm here for the foreseeable future."

I did not miss the way Maya's gaze snapped to me at that little nugget of information.

"What brings you to Meridel of all places?" Elsie asked.

Maya stiffened beside me, her head tilting, listening to my answer as she played with the ice cream on the plate.

"My mum lives close by. She spends half the year here to spend more time with her family, and the other half in England. I joined her last year, which was why I gave the photography class a try."

"You must be one heck of a photographer if you beat

Maya in that contest."

I was fully aware of the blush creeping back over Maya's cheeks, her eyes studying where she squeezed her hands in her lap.

Taking a chance, I grabbed one of Maya's hands, interlacing our fingers. "Maya is an incredible photographer. She easily should have won."

She didn't pull her hand away, though she was stiff as a board, her palm clammy.

Elsie narrowed her eyes at Maya before saying to me, "You're a lot nicer than Maya made you out to be."

"Um, thank you?"

Maya went rigid next to me. Then Elsie looked at me before I could process her words further. "Did Maya tell you? She entered that—"

"Okay!" Maya interrupted, squirming out of my grip. "Everyone done eating? We should really get going." Then she was out of the booth, shrugging on her coat while we all stared at her.

"Are you okay?" Elsie asked, her nose scrunching. "We haven't finished dessert yet."

"I, uh…bathroom!"

Before any of us could react, she half speed walked half sprinted to the corner of the restaurant. For a moment we all stared after her, unsure how to respond to her sudden freakout.

"Should I go check on her?" Elsie asked.

I shook my head. "I'll be right back."

Neither of them said a word as I slipped out of the booth and made my way to the bathrooms. I expected to have to wait outside in the hallway, but to my surprise Maya was standing in the dark corner next to the door, face in her hands.

"Maya?"

Her head snapped up, eyes wide.

It was dark in the hallway, but it looked like she might have been crying. Her cheeks were glistening.

"Hey, what's wrong?" I stopped in front of her, moving the hair out of her face. It was only natural for my fingers to skim down her cheek and neck. Her blue eyes glinted in the dim light as they met mine. "You know they love you and were just poking fun at you. And I didn't mean for the comment about the class competition to come across badly. I really think you—"

Her hand covered my mouth, silencing me. Sparks flitted over my face, down my arms, and all the way to my toes. Did she feel it when she touched me too, or was it all in my head?

"I'm okay, Oliver," she whispered. Her breath smelled like chocolate. "I just needed a minute."

I suspected that there was more to her explanation, but she didn't offer anything else. Part of me wanted to pry, to understand what was going on in the mind of this stunning woman that had been haunting my dreams for over a year, but the other part of me didn't want to do or say anything else that would bring tears to her eyes.

I wanted to *stop* her tears. Could I distract her? Make her smile?

What would she do if I kissed her? Surely *that* would be an adequate distraction.

Her hand slipped from my lips, her gaze never leaving mine.

"I was wondering about something Elsie said." I stepped closer. "It sounded like you've mentioned me before."

"You're my enemy. Of course, I've talked about you."

A mixed cocktail of pleasure and irritation spilled through me. I hated that she felt I was her enemy, but she had brought me up before...and that meant she was thinking about me.

I backed her toward the wall and planted my hands on either side of her. I leaned forward, my nose skimming along her neck, my beard brushing her ear. She sucked in a breath.

"Do you really think I'm your enemy, Maya?"

A shiver shuddered through her, and she closed her eyes. "I don't know what to think of you anymore," she admitted, her voice so quiet I thought I had imagined it. I took another step closer, our chests almost touching.

"Villain or hero...I'll be whatever you want if it keeps me close to you."

Her breath caught, and I was sure lightning was about to strike from all the tension crackling between us. What would she do if I kissed her?

No sooner had the thought passed through my mind than Elsie's voice shattered the moment. "There you are, we thought you—"

Elsie froze, noticing our proximity. I swallowed, wanting nothing more than to stay right here, but I forced my arms to return to my sides and wrangled my legs backward until there was an appropriate amount of space between us.

Maya looked at me with hooded eyes, like she was in a trance, before she blinked and cleared her throat, moving away from me.

"Sorry. I'm good. Let's get out of here."

Elsie and I stood stunned as Maya marched toward the door and fled the restaurant.

What just happened?

My mind was fuzzy like I had sipped on too many glasses of wine.

Was it possible to get love drunk? Not that this was love or anything...

"Keep rattling her, Oliver," Elsie spoke after a moment, pulling me from my thoughts.

"Pardon?"

She turned those brown eyes on me. "Keep shaking her up. Maya is one of a kind, but she pushes everyone away. She needs a good guy to get her out of that box she uses to keep herself safe."

I studied her as I processed her words.

"How do you know I'm a good guy?"

Elsie's laugh was light as she headed back to her fiancé, throwing over her shoulder, "Bad guys don't look at her the way you do."

13

Maya

The ghost of Oliver's hands on my skin haunted me all night long, keeping my dreams well in the "hot" and "more than friends" zone. I woke up multiple times, clothes sweaty, panting for breath, and I swore I could still feel his fingers lighting little fires along my skin.

I had no one to blame but myself. I shouldn't have let Oliver get so close in that hallway; should have never let him block me in or get within kissing distance.

Would I have kissed him if he had closed that inch of space between us? That was the question repeating over and over in my head, and the answer was even more infuriating: I didn't know.

By five in the morning, I was so sick of the dreams and spinning thoughts that I flung the blankets off with a growl and stomped into the kitchen to make some coffee.

Blast you, Oliver.

My hands trembled as I attempted to pour the coffee grounds into the filter, then spilled half its contents onto the counter when I tried to lift it into the coffee maker.

"Dang flabbit," I muttered, using my hand to scoop the grounds back into the filter. I wasn't about to waste a speck of this glorious brown dirt that made magic in a cup.

A minute later, I had coffee brewing away in the pot. I plopped down on my couch, glaring at nothing in particular. The combination of little sleep and being up early had me in a terrible mood.

At least I had today off work. That was a positive.

But now I was out of routine, which made me feel on edge. That was a negative.

I was up way too early, I had run out of my favorite peanut butter puff cereal since I still hadn't gotten groceries, and the spitting noise of the coffee maker as it finished brewing was getting on my last nerve.

I considered trying to go back to bed, but then a memory of dream Oliver's hands on my waist and in my hair made me quickly shut down that idea.

My phone buzzed on the end table, making me jump. A text lit up the screen, causing me to groan when I saw who it was from.

Speak of the devil.

BLASTED BRIT

Are you awake?

I snorted when Oliver's new contact name flashed on the screen, and I couldn't help typing a snarky response.

ME

You've reached the ghost of Maya.

She is no longer here. Please don't leave a message. Farewell.

BLASTED BRIT

Hello, Maya's ghost. Why are you up so early?

ME

I think you missed the point of not leaving a message.

BLASTED BRIT

I'm nothing if not persistent.

ME

That's one word for it.

What do you want, Oliver?

BLASTED BRIT

Not a morning person. Got it.

Are you busy today?

ME

I don't think you've earned the right to
know whether I'm busy or not.

BLASTED BRIT

That has yet to be determined, but your BOYFRIEND
should know whether you have today off from work.

ME

Good thing you're not actually my boyfriend.

BLASTED BRIT

Don't you think we should work on that?

For a moment, my heart dropped into my stomach.

BLASTED BRIT

Elsie is right, Maya. If we can't even convince her,
there's no way my father will believe we're dating.

He was right, but the thought of spending more time
with him while being close and touchy made my hands
slick with sweat. The way Oliver had treated me lately
had left me confused, questioning all the hate I had ever
felt for him.

Sure, he still teased me, but instead of mean, it felt
more...flirtatious. I found myself struggling to remember
if perhaps this was how it always was, and maybe I had

misinterpreted it. But, then again, maybe Oliver was just good at faking.

I was so tired of the strange way this man was making me feel that I almost called the whole thing off. I wanted to say, "sorry but I changed my mind. I don't want to fake date you anymore." My fingers slammed against the screen as I typed out the message, but a single thought had my thumb pausing above the send button.

If I called off the fake dating, there went any chance of meeting Oliver's dad, and thus my chance at a possible advantage in winning that photography competition.

As much as I hated the idea of spending more time with Oliver, and dealing with this weird way he kept making me feel, the need to win that prize money was too great. I couldn't back out now.

ME

rolling eyes emoji

You're insufferable, British man.

BLASTED BRIT

But you secretly like it.

Even if you won't admit it to yourself.

That odd fluttering sensation filled my stomach again and I swallowed it down, sending:

ME

I have today off.

BLASTED BRIT

Excellent. Pick you up in an hour.

"Are. You. Kidding. Me?"

It was just past eight, we'd spent two hours driving across Iowa to some unknown destination, and my travel mug ran out of coffee ninety minutes ago.

"Are you kidding me?" I repeated, glaring at Oliver as we sat in his Jeep. "Why would you bring me here?"

Oliver's deep chuckle had goosebumps rising over my arms as he pulled a black knit cap over his head and slid his hands into a pair of gloves. "You needed some Christmas cheer."

"So, you brought me to a Christmas tree farm?" I shrieked, my voice far too shrill for the confines of the car. "What? Has Christmas always been sunshine and daisies for you so you feel the need to shove it down my throat, too?"

Oliver took it in stride, not even wincing at my hysterics. "On the contrary, Christmas has never been easy in my family, but you need this. You could use a little Christmas magic."

I crossed my arms, ignoring the bright flare of curiosity in the back of my mind. What had Oliver meant about his family Christmases?

"There's no such thing. Take me back home, Oliver. I didn't agree to this."

"I'm afraid I can't do that, Maya. Put on your happy pants and get moving."

"Unfortunately for you, the store was all out of happy pants last time I was there. They only had crabby panties."

My head shook in a violent motion. "Besides, the joke is on you because my apartment building doesn't allow real trees." I fought the urge to stick my tongue out at him.

Oliver's smile was blinding. "Who said it was for you? The tree is for *my* home. You're just helping me pick one out." He climbed out of the car, leaving me gaping before scrambling after him. The scent of evergreen and pine was overwhelming.

"I tell you I don't do Christmas and your first thought is to force me to go Christmas tree shopping?" I spit at him, after running to catch up.

"Precisely."

I had to shove my hands into my coat pockets to keep from smacking him. "Are you kidding me?"

Oliver slowed and looked down at me. "Perhaps we should work on broadening your vocabulary next."

A frustrated scream built in my throat, and I bit my

lip to hold it back. My eyes burned, and I hated that I was reacting this way to something so simple. Why couldn't he just accept that I didn't celebrate Christmas and leave it at that? Why was he forcing me into this?

A gloved hand grabbed my arm and pulled me to a stop before Oliver's blue eyes were piercing into mine.

"Maya, this isn't just about Christmas trees, is it?"

I couldn't answer him even if I wanted to. My breaths were like jagged knives slicing up my throat as I struggled for each breath, clouding in the cold air.

Oliver's mitten slid up and down my arm, and even though there were several layers between us, it sent waves of calm through my body.

"Maya," he whispered, stepping closer before he pulled me against his chest and wrapped his arms around my waist. His chin pressed against the top of my head. For a moment, I stood there shocked, my arms hanging at my sides before I finally wound them around him.

"What are you doing?" I muttered into his coat, ignoring the fact that I was hugging him back.

"Holding you."

"Why?"

Oliver's chest heaved under my face, and I wasn't sure if he was laughing or sighing.

"I'm trying to comfort you."

Though the words were spoken in English, they sounded like gibberish, and I had a difficult time comprehending them. Outside of Elsie or Emma, I couldn't recall the last time someone had just held me when I was upset. Guys tended to run the other way, not pull me closer.

Snowflakes fell in lazy circles around us as minutes passed, and Oliver didn't let go. We were the only two at the tree farm aside from the tired-looking teenager nursing a coffee in the red shed across the parking lot. Clearly, everyone else had the sense to stay in bed. Or at least at home.

Oliver's heat seeped into me, warming me despite the winter day. His nose pressed into my hair for a moment before he shifted his weight.

"Maya...please tell me why you don't celebrate Christmas."

I squeezed my eyes shut, wishing that I could disappear. I hated talking about this, about anything to do with my family. People always looked at me either like something was wrong with me for my parents to have abandoned me, or worse, like I was broken and needed their pity.

I pulled out of Oliver's arms, but he gripped my shoulders, not letting me escape far. He brushed my hair behind one ear. His blue eyes held none of what I feared—there was no pity or a look that told me he thought I was damaged, just a genuine desire to know why I hated Christmas.

"I won't force you to tell me, Maya, but...I want to understand. Christmas is such a special time of year. I want to know why it's not for you."

A shaky breath shuddered out of me. As much as I

didn't want to open up to my archnemesis, I had held all of it in for so long that it was like water bursting through a cracked dam. I couldn't hold back the flood of words.

"My dad abandoned us when I was a kid. One night he was there, tucking me into bed, and when I woke up the next morning, he was gone." I lowered my gaze to Oliver's chest, unable to look him in the eye.

"My mom told me that he didn't love us enough to stay. After that..." I paused before sighing, not wanting to share the entire sob story in the middle of a tree farm. "Let's just say my mom wasn't around much afterward, leaving me to celebrate holidays on my own...at least until my cousins started inviting me to spend it with them a few years ago."

I dared a glance at Oliver, terrified that he would let go of his grip on me and turn his back, deciding I was too much to deal with.

Oliver's glove trailed across my cheek, and he was quiet for another moment. "I'm sorry, Maya."

I sniffled. Oliver pulled me back into him, his gloved hands sliding around my back. "You deserve more."

Though I hadn't shared the full story of how my mom became a workaholic after my dad left, of how she cared more about her career than me, my body loosened after speaking the words aloud. Why had I waited so long to tell someone? I had carried a weight the size of Texas on my shoulders for years, made even heavier by shame and anxiety, but in just a few words, that weight, that ache, had lifted.

I could breathe again.

Oliver's hand brushed the hair from my face, settling on my neck. He took a deep breath.

"In all the pain, I think you've forgotten something special about Christmas though. It's not about the people that *aren't* there but the people that *are*. You have many people who love and care about you. Celebrate with *them* instead and forget about all the things you've lost. Make new memories. Enjoy this time of year *in spite* of whatever pain is associated with the holiday. If you focus on the pain, that's all you'll ever feel, but if you focus on the joy, the pain will ease, and you'll find the happiness you've been waiting for."

He removed his gloves and trailed his fingers down my cheek. "I want to help you find that spark of joy again."

My stomach awoke with butterflies, so powerful they threatened to burst through my skin. A single word slipped through my lips.

"Why?"

I didn't understand why Oliver Lewis, my real-life villain, wanted to help me find my happy.

Oliver's throat bobbed as he swallowed, his blue eyes wide behind his glasses. "Because—"

"Howdy, folks!" a man's voice called across the parking lot. A ridiculously tall man strode toward us, his shoulders so broad that I wondered how he even fit through doorways.

Oliver and I pulled apart. Regret swirled in his eyes over not saying whatever he'd been about to say.

The man stopped in front of us and stuck his hand out. "The name's Leaf. I own this here tree farm! Do you two need any help picking one out?"

A beat of silence.

"Your name is *Leaf* and you own a *tree* farm," I deadpanned, ignoring his question.

The man didn't miss a beat, laughing so loud my ears rang. "Ironic, ain't it?"

Oliver chuckled. "We were just browsing, sir."

Leaf eyed the two of us. "Well, as lovely as this lady's eyes are, you won't find the perfect Christmas tree there." My cheeks burned as he turned on his heel, heading for the row of trees that had yet to be cut down. "Come on, I'll show you my pride and joy."

"I sure hope he means the trees," Oliver whispered into my ear, and I had to cover my mouth to keep my laugh inside.

"Did you just...make a joke, Oliver?"

He winked. "There's a lot you have to learn about me, darling."

The breath caught in my throat at the term of endearment. Why would he call me that? And what had he been about to say before we were interrupted?

Oliver slipped his glove back on and wrapped his hand around mine.

"Come on, we better follow him before he picks us up and carries us himself."

Oliver

Leaf led us up and down row after row of evergreen trees until I was certain that the smell would forever be ingrained in my nose hairs.

I didn't mind, I loved all things Christmas, but Leaf had cut through my plans like *I* was a tree to chop down. I had wanted to spend the morning perusing the tree selection with Maya, maybe get her to tell me more about herself, and if I was lucky, steal a few kisses beneath the trees.

But the blasted tree man just kept walking and talking like we were the only two people on the planet he could possibly talk to.

I guess this is what you get for arriving right when they opened.

One thing was for sure. The man *adored* his trees. He'd been talking for an entire hour without running out of things to tell us or stories to share. Maya had a pleasant smile on her face the entire time, and I wasn't sure if she was humoring him or if she enjoyed learning everything there was to know about pine trees.

After another ten minutes, I couldn't take it anymore. I needed time with Maya without tree man stealing her attention.

I cleared my throat. "Thank you for the tour, Leaf, and all the knowledge you shared about your trees. I think the lady and I will peruse on our own for a while and see if we can't find the right one to fit in our space."

Did I purposefully make it sound like we were together and picking one out for our shared place?

Yes. Yes, I did.

Maya gave me the side eye while I just smiled.

Leaf seemed surprised that we wouldn't need his help and sputtered for a moment before taking a step back. "Well, of course. Take your time and let me know if you have any questions for me." He looked very much like he hoped we had more questions.

Poor guy.

Instead of walking back down the row, Leaf literally walked *into* the trees, disappearing beneath the boughs.

Maya sighed and whispered, "Is he really gone?" She watched the branches for any sign of movement.

"I think so. He probably went to the Under-tree-world."

Maya snorted at my lame attempt at a joke, and I couldn't keep the dorky grin from my face.

"You should've gotten rid of him sooner," she said.

"What? You mean you *didn't* want to learn about how you can gauge humidity in the air by looking at pine cones?"

Maya snorted. "I don't need to look at pine cones when the state of my hair will tell me all I need to know."

"Your hair is perfect." I froze as the words passed my lips. That was meant to be an inside thought.

Maya stilled, looking at me quizzically. "What?"

I scrambled to think of a response, but the only thing that came out was, "What?"

Maya arched a brow, staring at me as if I'd lost my mind. Maybe I had.

Being around her had my heart, and mind for that matter, doing strange things.

I swallowed, gesturing down the row. "Come on, there was one down here that might be perfect."

"Like my hair?" she taunted.

She was baiting me, but I could play along. I reached out and gently tugged her soft, blonde hair.

"Precisely. Though the tree is admittedly not as beautiful."

A pink tint rose in Maya's cheeks, and she looked away, avoiding my gaze.

Oliver: 1, Maya: 0

With a smug smile, I wandered down the row, searching for the tree that had caught my eye earlier. When I located it, I grabbed Maya's hand in mine, and pulled her to the last one on the left.

At first, Maya was speechless.

"*That's* the one you want?"

I admired the wonky tree. It was slightly crooked, half of it was smooshed, and it was missing a large amount of pine needles. It was on the smaller side, too, but I didn't mind.

"This is the one," I confirmed.

Maya looked at all the other trees around us. "But... why?"

The corner of my mouth pulled up in a smirk. "Things don't need to be flawless to be beautiful."

She cocked her head, thinking through my words as if such a concept had never occurred to her.

"Some things are beautiful simply because they exist. They don't have to try, they don't have to work and strive and struggle. None of that means anything when they're incredible just for the simple fact that they're alive."

I paused, brushing my glove over the missing needles. "Besides, sometimes you just need to give what you have a chance instead of always searching for something that might be better. You'll never be content that way."

Maya's ice-blue gaze snapped to mine. "You're a lot deeper than I expected."

I shrugged. "Some people will surprise you if you let them."

Her breath pooled in the cold air as she exhaled, and

she shoved her hands into her coat pockets. She seemed a little unsure—whether of herself or my words, I didn't know. Had I rendered her speechless?

Despite the steady fall of snow, the tree farm had grown busier, people milling about amongst the trees. Small children ran back and forth, hiding from their parents beneath the boughs, and Leaf's booming laugh echoed all the way from the parking lot. We hadn't had much of a chance for "practicing" being a couple since Leaf hijacked the first hour of our visit. All the ways I had hoped this spontaneous adventure would turn out hadn't happened, but our fake date/Christmas spirit trip wasn't over yet.

"So, this is the one then?" Maya asked, nodding at the special tree.

Just as I opened my mouth to answer, another voice spoke.

"How are the two lovebirds doing over here? Have you selected a tree?" Leaf asked, appearing out of nowhere.

Lovebirds? Really Leaf?

Maya sniggered under her breath, and I replied with a smile, "We have. We'll take this one." I pointed to the sad looking tree.

Leaf blinked at it for several moments before his brow wrinkled. "This one? Are you...are you sure? We have much nicer—"

"Positive." No one was going to talk me out of this ugly tree.

"Well…I…" he sighed, rubbing at the back of his neck. "Alrighty then. I'll be right back to cut it down for you."

Leaf turned on his heel and disappeared down the snowy path so fast I would have assumed his pants were on fire.

"I dare you to pretend this is real," I whispered to Maya once he was gone, stepping closer to her.

"Huh?" She turned confused eyes on me.

"We haven't gotten to practice being a real couple since Leaf gave us special treatment. I dare you to put on your best faking pants to convince Leaf and everyone else here how in love with me you are."

Maya's throat bobbed as she swallowed, but then she gave a single nod. "Okay, I accept your *dare*, Oliver. But just remember that it's all fake. I don't mean any of it."

Ouch. The words punched straight through my gut.

"Here we are!" Leaf announced as he jumped through the line of trees like a child, brandishing a long saw.

I leaned in so my lips brushed against Maya's ear, and I didn't miss the way she shivered.

"It's showtime."

Maya

At his taunting words, all inhibitions fled my mind as I threw myself into his side and wrapped my arms around his waist. Oliver stumbled back from the force of it, his chest moving in a silent laugh.

"I'm not sure that tackling me counts as affection," he whispered.

Heat burned my cheeks despite the cold air, and I squeezed him harder in retaliation for his teasing, feeling satisfied when he coughed.

"Aren't you two just the bee's knees?" Leaf commented before preparing to saw down Oliver's pitiful tree.

"The bee's knees? What era is he from?" I muttered.

Oliver pinched my side, eliciting a startled yelp from me.

There was a playfulness in Oliver's eyes that I hadn't seen before, and it spurred me to lean onto my tippy toes and peck a kiss on his cheek. I had never felt so much pleasure from watching someone's eyes widen in surprise. His gloved hand touched his cheek where I had kissed it like he couldn't believe I had done such a thing.

With a devilish smile, I pulled away from him. I thought it would be awkward pretending to like him, but I had to admit that I enjoyed getting under his skin and making Oliver Lewis unsettled for once.

The sound of Leaf sawing away at the tree trunk filled the air, distracting me as fat snowflakes swirled in the sky, falling heavier by the minute. The owner of the tree farm whistled an off-key version of "We Wish You a Merry Christmas" as he finished sawing and then yelled, "Timber!" obnoxiously loud when it was just the two of us nearby.

The tree barely made a thud on the ground.

Why the heck did Oliver choose that sad little thing?

"Ahem," a voice said, snapping me out of the silent pity party I was having for the tree.

I looked over my shoulder to find Oliver behind me, his eyes flickering with amusement.

"I know my tree is cute and all but staring at it and ignoring me isn't convincing anyone that you love me."

"But I don't love you," I whispered back. It was an automatic response, drilled into my brain by my waning hatred for Oliver Lewis. Something flashed in his eyes, and it almost looked like…hurt.

He blinked whatever the emotion was away and smirked, his beard scratching against my ear again as he leaned in. "No one else knows that."

I sighed, knowing there was no way out of this. I had to keep acting or I risked Oliver calling the whole thing off. I should've known that a tackle and a cheek kiss wouldn't be enough for him.

Swallowing the flutters in my stomach, I grabbed Oliver's hand. There, I was holding his hand. Surely that was good enough, right? Couples held hands all the time.

Oliver snorted. "Is that your idea of affection?"

"I'm holding your hand. What more do you want?"

As if my words were a challenge, a spark flashed in his eyes, and he tugged my arm so that I was in front of him, my back to his chest. Then he wrapped his arms around my waist, resting his chin on the top of my head.

"*This* is what couples do," he murmured. "None of that teenage holding hands stuff."

"Hey, there's nothing wrong with holding your hand."

"Maybe not, but you won't convince *anyone* that we're in love with that."

I sighed, my breath clouding the air. I hated that he was right, but it was hard to get past my reservations about him and put on a show. I was hesitant, not because I hated him, but because I was afraid of what would happen to my feelings if I took things further.

I didn't want to have feelings for Oliver Lewis. I had

my future to think about—there wasn't time for feelings. Besides, I wasn't about to risk my heart when the two people who were supposed to love me the most had abandoned me.

Oliver would be no different. He'd go back to England, leaving me behind. My life was here. Letting myself develop feelings for him would be dangerous. And touching and pretending to be a couple confused that determination to keep my distance.

But even so, pretending to be in love with my enemy was much easier than it should've been.

Trying to rewire my brain to not think Oliver was a villain was hard but hating him was no longer feeling natural. It almost required more effort to continue despising him.

But even more frustrating than finding it difficult to hate Oliver was that faking the *physical* part of the relationship was...natural. The more I touched him, fell into him, even pulling our gloves off to lace my fingers between his...it was all as easy as breathing.

Even the jolt that went through me at our skin touching felt normal.

But that was absurd because I didn't even *like* Oliver Lewis.

...Right?

I'd been so convinced that Oliver was a terrible person, taking what he wanted, when he wanted, without regard for anyone else. Never had I expected there to be a decent person beneath that smug smile and those Clark Kent glasses. Never would I have expected to encounter the deep and kind man that he was proving to be.

But I had to remember that I was just using him to gain an advantage in the photography competition. None of this was real. It couldn't be.

Not even if the warmth of Oliver's arms around me, holding me tight, was one of the best things I had experienced in years.

"I'll have this wrapped up in a jiffy and I'll meet you over by your car to help get it secured," Leaf announced, ripping me from my thoughts as he pulled out a long spool of red string.

Oliver nodded his appreciation before guiding me back to the parking lot. He hadn't released his hold on me.

"We're not seriously going to walk all the way back there like this," I said, irritated. Our boots kept getting tangled together as we walked.

"Why not?"

I looked up at him. "This is ridiculous. Let me go."

Challenge flashed in his eyes. "As you wish."

The weight of his arms disappeared, and I fell face first into the snow.

I wanted to scream. I wanted to laugh. I wanted to smack the smug smile off Oliver's face.

"What the heck was that?" I cried, flipping over to glare at him.

"You said let go."

I pushed to my feet and got in his face. "You weren't supposed to let me fall on my face!"

His smirk said he was enjoying this way too much. He shrugged. "You said let go. You didn't ask me to catch you."

"Are you kidding?"

"I see we're back to that question again."

I groaned, wanting to pull my hair out. "You are incredible."

"Thanks, so are you."

I stopped dead in my tracks and fixed the most intense glare I could muster. I wouldn't even allow myself to examine that compliment.

I brushed the snow off my coat and pants in exasperated movements, my blood burning beneath my skin.

"Who do you think you are?" I snapped quietly, but of course he heard it.

"I'll catch you when you ask me to," he answered.

I gaped at his audacity.

And then Oliver stepped closer so that our boots were touching, and my angry, heaving chest was mere inches from his. He brushed my hair over my shoulder, his fingers trailing a line of fire down my neck. "Next time you're falling, Maya, I won't drop you. All you have to do is ask."

My heart squeezed, my stomach flip-flopping. He was so close, that sweet, smoky scent of his cologne smothering my senses, and I leaned into him. His blue eyes were a cage that I was willingly locking myself in.

"Well, now!" Leaf exclaimed, interrupting whatever moment we were having, and we both flinched and sprung apart. Leaf pointed above our heads. "Mistletoe!"

The blood drained from my face and my stomach fell to the snowy earth beneath my feet.

"We're not really into public displays of affection," I said, wracking my brain for any way to get out of kissing Oliver in front of a Christmas tree farm full of people. Holding hands and kissing his cheek was one thing, but *actually* kissing Oliver?

That was a line there was no coming back from once crossed.

"Rules are rules," Leaf half sang, pointing to the green plant hanging above us that spelled my doom.

"Now's your chance to convince everyone this is real," Oliver said, too low for anyone but me to hear.

My breath caught as he stepped close to me, wrapping his hand around my waist and pulling me toward him. Panic filled my stomach, burning up my throat like acid reflux.

I couldn't kiss Oliver Lewis. If I crossed that line, there was no telling what would happen next. For all I knew, all my hatred for the man holding me would pop like a balloon, escaping into the air like helium.

Oliver's lips twitched with amusement as he leaned toward me. His eyes seemed to say, *let's give them a show.*

But before he touched his lips to mine, he must have

seen the terror in my eyes because he hesitated and twisted me to the side. I expected warm lips to touch mine, but instead, they grazed the very corner of my mouth. The angle at which he moved me made it appear as though he gave me a solid kiss, but the two of us knew it wasn't a kiss at all.

Though his lips barely touched mine, they were as warm as I imagined—not that I imagined kissing him.

A weird sinking feeling filled my gut as he pulled back, his eyes no longer full of amusement but something like reservation. Had I hurt him by not wanting to kiss him? I *hadn't* wanted him to kiss me—at least not here in front of Leaf under a mistletoe—so why was I filled with disappointment too?

Oliver's hands slipped from my waist, releasing me, and he stepped back. Leaf and an older couple gave a few enthusiastic claps as if our fake kiss was the greatest Broadway show they'd ever seen. The onlookers dispersed, leaving us staring at each other.

I cleared my throat, brushing the snow from my coat. "We should get going," I said, looking at the sky and wincing when a snowflake landed in my eye. "The weather is getting worse, and I don't want to get stuck driving back home."

Oliver studied my face for a moment, and I feared he'd ask what my problem was, why kissing him was such a big deal, but then his eyes shuttered, and that infernal smirk made its return. "Oh, ye of little faith. My Jeep will have no problem in the snow."

And just like that, our fake not-a-kiss and whatever we both felt as a result was shoved into a box, neither of us willing to address it now.

I swallowed. "Just because it *can* drive in the snow doesn't mean it should. I'd rather not risk driving two hours on bad roads."

Oliver put his hands up in surrender. "All right. Let me pay for the tree first, then we'll head home."

Why did Oliver calling Meridel home do strange things to my insides?

Ten minutes later, after strapping the tree to the roof of the Jeep and a lengthy goodbye from Leaf, we were nice and warm in Oliver's car, driving on the snowy roads back to Meridel. It was a good thing we left when we did because it was already slippery and difficult to see where the lanes on the road were.

Oliver appeared at ease as he drove with one hand on the steering wheel and the other arm draped across the center console. His fingers tapped the rhythm of whatever electronic dance music he had turned on. I had never listened to that type of music before, but I found myself bobbing along with it, my foot tapping against the mat beneath my feet.

Thirty minutes later, the wind was whipping the snow in a thick blanket that was impossible to see through. There was no road anymore, just faint tire tracks through the snow.

"I don't like this," I muttered. I had always hated driving in the snow, especially on country roads that weren't plowed. But this wasn't just snow. This was a blizzard.

My heart pounded against my chest, and I squeezed my hands together in my lap.

Oliver looked at me, brows lowering over his eyes. Maybe I hadn't been as quiet as I thought. His knuckles were now white on the steering wheel.

"Maya," Oliver said, breaking my concentration from the nonexistent road.

"Eyes on the road!" I snapped, terrified that we'd swerve into a ditch if he looked at me for even a moment.

"What road?"

"Exactly!"

Oliver chuckled. How was he so calm right now? Any moment we could drive off the invisible road into a ditch and he looked unbothered by that possibility. Meanwhile, my lungs were constricting, forcing any ounce of air out, and I couldn't breathe.

"Maya, do you trust me?" Oliver's voice was calm, but it did nothing to soothe my fear.

"Absolutely not." The words were out of my mouth before I could think, and they burned my tongue.

He cocked his head. "Well, I need you to trust me."

Uh-oh. That doesn't sound good.

"Why?"

Oliver sighed. "I think we should pull over and wait

out the storm."

"What?" My shout filled the Jeep, and I winced at how loud it was.

He didn't bother to respond before slowing the car even more. Someone's driveway appeared on the right, the path so long you couldn't see the house in the distance through the snow, and he pulled onto it before putting the car into park.

"We're off the main road, so hopefully no one will slide into us. We'll stay here until it lightens up enough to drive back to town."

Then Oliver turned the car off. I swear my heart stuttered to a stop in my chest.

"Oh my gosh." My breaths were short gasps and it felt like there was a hive of bees in my chest. "We're going to freeze to death. We're going to die on the side of the road in the middle of nowhere and no one will ever find our bodies and—"

Oliver pressed a finger to my lips, silencing me. I blinked at him.

"Maya, everything's okay."

"Okay?" I asked against his finger. "How is being stuck on the side of the road in a blizzard remotely close to okay?"

Oliver pulled his hand away, and I fought the urge to grab it and hold on for dear life.

"We're not stuck, we're just choosing to wait out the storm. We're fine. I have blankets in the back and a bag of emergency supplies. I've got it covered."

I crossed my arms over my chest, wishing the pressure would ease the ache settling in like a bone-numbing cold.

"I'll keep driving if you want me to, Maya, but I think it's better if we wait it out."

As much as I hated the idea of being stranded on the side of the road for hours in a snowstorm with Oliver, driving on these treacherous roads when we couldn't see even a few feet in front of the car was foolish.

Waiting it out was the best decision.

But that meant I was stuck in close quarters with Oliver for an untold number of hours. And *that* terrified me, especially since I wasn't sure I hated him anymore.

"Fine," I muttered, pulling the hood of my coat down over my face.

Oliver's chuckle warmed my bones against the chill that was already settling in the car. I fished my phone out of my coat pocket intending to distract myself from the man next to me, but I didn't have a signal.

Great. I can't even pretend he's not here.

His sweet pipe tobacco scent filled the Jeep. Maybe I shouldn't have agreed to wait out the storm. If I was stuck in close proximity with him and that cologne, I was done for.

I could not be held accountable for my actions— whatever they may be.

I peeked at Oliver who stared at his own phone, brow furrowed.

"No signal," I said, shutting off my phone to save the battery before chucking it into the cup holder.

Oliver opened his door, resulting in a burst of cold air and snow flying into the car.

"What the heck are you doing?" I cried, burrowing deeper into my coat, and he shut the door again.

Oliver just laughed. "I'm grabbing the stuff from the back, so Your Royal Highness doesn't freeze to death."

I scoffed. "Royal Highness?"

"Well, you're acting like a spoiled princess so I might as well call you one."

"Surely you can be more creative than that."

"I could've gone with brat, but that felt a little mean."

I gasped, searching the Jeep for something I could throw at him, but of course the car was spotless.

Oliver's laugh had goosebumps raising on my arms. "I'm just teasing you, princess. I'll be right back."

I'd be lying if I said that him calling me princess didn't have my stomach doing somersaults.

He slipped out of the car and opened the trunk, rummaging around for a few seconds. After he found whatever he was looking for, he got back into the car. But instead of getting back in the driver's seat, Oliver crawled into the backseat.

"Um, what are you doing?" I asked.

Oliver handed me a thick blanket before pulling a big black bag into his lap. He fished out a bottle of water and some pretzels and offered them to me. I took them with shaking hands. "Thanks."

He shrugged. "It never hurts to be prepared for anything. Those pretzels might be expired, but at least it'll fill your belly."

"Or empty it," I muttered beneath my breath. "Why are you in the backseat?"

He stretched his arms out to either side, then propped his boots up onto the center console. "Lots more room back here. If I'm stuck in the Jeep for hours, might as well be comfortable." Then, to my horror, he patted the seat next to him. "Plenty of room for two."

I gave a violent shake of my head. "No way, Oliver."

His lips twisted into a smirk. "What? Afraid I'll bite?"

Yes, something like that. My lips, my neck...stop it, Maya!

My face must have betrayed my inner thoughts because he crossed his arms, his gaze burning with something that looked a lot like desire. But I was just imagining that, right?

"Don't worry, Maya. I'll keep my hands to myself unless you ask for otherwise. I'm simply offering you body heat. It'll be cold in here soon. This is survival—nothing more." His words made sense, but the look in his eyes made me think he wanted to add *unless you want more.*

Facing forward, I crossed my arms over my chest, choosing to ignore Oliver and the warmth he promised. I would have to be frozen solid before I took him up on that offer.

"Suit yourself." Oliver wrapped himself in another blanket and pulled a book out of his bag.

Oliver Lewis was a *reader*? He just got a million bonus points from Elsie for that.

Silence filled the Jeep aside from the faintest patter of snow hitting the windows. I lasted all of twenty minutes before the cold was unbearable and my entire body shivered from head to toe.

"You're shaking the car, Maya."

I closed my eyes, pretending to be asleep.

"Come on, Maya. I can't stand seeing you sitting there freezing. Come back here. Let me warm you up. I promise to be good."

Any chance at pretending to be asleep died as I let out a loud, "Ha!"

"What?" He gave me a blank look.

"You promise to be good? Yeah, right."

Oliver's gaze softened. "I don't want you to suffer. I'm just offering to keep you warm, so we don't freeze while we wait."

Why did my stomach swoop at the thought of letting Oliver hold me?

"Come on."

I wanted to say no. I didn't want to risk what *I* might do if I crawled into the back and cuddled with him.

But my teeth chattered, and my body ached from how hard it was shaking. The snow had shown no signs of letting up, so there was no telling how long we'd be stranded here. As stubborn as I was, I didn't think I'd be able to hold out.

It was just too cold.

"Fine," I muttered before throwing my blanket in the back. I awkwardly threw my legs over the center console to slide between the seats, then plopped down next to Oliver.

He wasted no time scooting closer and wrapping his blanket around both of us.

I pushed it away. "I can use my own blanket."

"But mine is already warm, making it easier to share body heat."

I sighed, too cold to argue, and let him wrap us in the blanket. At first, he stayed shoulder-to-shoulder with me, but after a few minutes, when I hadn't stopped shaking, he let out a sigh of his own.

"I'm going to put my arms around you, okay? You'll never get warm unless I hold you."

"T-that's a l-line if I've ever heard o-one," I stuttered through chattering teeth.

Oliver huffed a laugh. "I promised no funny business." He paused, looking me in the eye. "Unless you *want* funny business."

I rolled my eyes. "Just warm me up, Oliver." A mischievous grin spread across his face. "Nicely."

His smile defied physical bounds. "There's lots of ways to warm you up *nicely*."

Heat flooded me as I blushed, and I shoved his shoulder.

He laughed. "Okay, okay. Lean forward."

I arched a brow at him but did as he said. Oliver adjusted the blanket before laying down behind me. His hands spread across my stomach, inviting me to lay in front of him.

Desperate for warmth, I laid down, and his arms wound around me, pressing me into him as he settled the blanket around us. Heat engulfed me, and I let out a shuddering sigh.

"Better?" he crooned in my ear, eliciting a shiver that had nothing to do with the cold.

I nodded, not trusting whatever might come out of my mouth next.

It was awkward with the two of us on the seat like this. Oliver was too tall, his shoulders a little too broad for him to be comfortable, but he didn't complain once as he held me to him, his fingers trailing calming lines over my stomach.

My body relaxed as his heat seeped into me, a type of lullaby that had me fading into a warm slumber in the backseat of Oliver's Jeep.

Oliver

I blinked my eyes open, the frigid air smothering my face, though it was easy to ignore when I was curled under a warm blanket with the woman of my dreams. The front of my shirt was damp with sweat from where Maya's back was pressed against my stomach; her breathing slow and even, still asleep.

I smiled to myself. Maya had fallen asleep in my arms.

It shouldn't have made me as happy as it did, but inside I was positively giddy.

For over a year I had kept my crush on Maya hidden, but I'd always been dreaming of times like this. Days where I could surprise her with a fun date, like Christmas tree hunting, or fall asleep cuddled together. Though, admittedly, I never imagined we'd be stuck on the side of the road during a blizzard while cuddling, but hey. I wasn't about to complain.

My face was nuzzled into her neck, the fruity scent of her perfume doing wild things to my insides. I hadn't planned on falling asleep, but the longer I laid there, the more the heat from Maya's body relaxed my muscles, and my eyelids grew heavy. It didn't take long before I had followed her into dreamland.

The cold air smothered my face as I lifted my head to look around. The windows were fogged over and covered in snow, making the interior of the car dim. A thick layer of snow blanketed the car, and I could barely make out that it was still daylight, though it appeared dusk was quickly approaching. We must have slept for *hours*.

The sound of the wind whipping against the Jeep had ceased, and I wondered if the storm had let up enough to drive back home.

Maya's blonde hair was splayed out over the seat, her head propped up on the other blanket. Her lips were parted, and my mind flitted back to the tree farm where I had fake kissed her under the mistletoe.

Panic had flashed in her eyes when I leaned in, and it had taken everything in me to only peck the very corner of her lips. It wasn't a kiss at all, but it would have looked like one to everyone that had been watching. I still wished it had been real. I fought the urge to press my lips to her cheek as she slept.

I needed to get up soon, check out how much snow had fallen, and see if it was safe to get back on the road. At the thought of leaving this warm little bubble we had created, my arms tightened around Maya.

She shifted, then muttered something unintelligible, her eyes moving behind her lids.

Then the last thing I ever expected came out of her mouth.

"Oliver," she breathed, her head tilting to the side.

I froze, gobsmacked at what I'd heard. Did she wake up after all? I glanced over her shoulder and confirmed she was asleep. My heart skipped a beat; she'd said my name in her sleep.

Was Maya...dreaming about me?

She shifted backward, pushing into me, and I had to press my lips to her coat to hold back a groan.

Half of me wanted to let her sleep, to see if she would say anything else in her dream, but the other half wanted to wake her up and find out what she was dreaming about for her to say my name.

I was saved from making the decision when she suddenly flinched in my arms, her eyes popping open.

"Maya?" I dared to ask, and she jumped, as though she had forgotten I was there. She craned her head over her shoulder. Her pupils were wide, and her breath puffed out in little clouds.

"Oliver?" she asked, dazed. She wiggled around until she was facing me, her mouth inches from mine.

Maya was so close; it would only take a tiny movement for my lips would be on hers. I wanted it so badly, but I had promised her I wouldn't touch her unless she asked. I would hold true to my word, even though every part of me screamed to kiss her.

"Hey, sleepyhead. What were you dreaming about?"

Maya looked at me through hooded eyes. Was she still half asleep, or was she purposely looking at me like she was about to jump me? Or maybe that was just wishful thinking again. My brain was a jumbled mess with her so close.

Then her eyes flicked to my lips.

"Maya?" I breathed. Was she inching closer? Or was that me?

What is happening?

Maya's hand moved to my cheek.

Then she kissed me.

Maya Beck, the woman I'd secretly fancied for over a year, that I had dreamed of kissing countless times, was kissing *me*.

Throwing caution to the wind, I leaned into it, pulling her flush against me. Her lips were as soft as I had imagined.

We lost ourselves in the kiss, her fingers in my hair and mine around her back, when she pulled back with a gasp, almost falling off the seat. She put a hand to her mouth, her eyes wide as saucers.

"That must have been some dream," I commented,

and her cheeks went red as a rose. I dared to brush her hair back as she blinked at me.

"I'm sorry," she said, still covering her mouth.

"I'm not." *In fact, I'd like to do it again.*

She shook her head and a flood of frigid air slammed into me as she whipped off the blanket and sat up, putting her face in her hands.

"Hey," I said, sitting up next to her, ignoring my protesting muscles, cramped after being in one position for so long. I pulled her hair away from her face so I could see her. "What's wrong?"

Maya shook her head again. "I'm so embarrassed."

"Why?"

"Because I just threw myself at you! Like a...like—"

Her breaths were coming faster and faster, sounding like she was going to hyperventilate.

"Maya," I soothed. "Look at me."

Her sniffle threatened to undo me. I took her face in my hands.

"Maya, I don't regret that kiss for even a moment. Please don't be embarrassed."

She sniffled again, looking at me with glassy eyes. "You don't?"

"I'd happily do it again to show you just how much I *don't* regret it."

Maya rolled her eyes with a scoff, but the corners of her mouth twitched as she fought a smile.

"I must know though...*what* were you dreaming

about?”

"Do I even need to tell you?" She tucked her hair behind an ear. "Didn't that tell you enough?"

"Well, when something gets me kissed like *that*, I'd like to know what it was." A slow smile spread across my face. "Do you often have naughty dreams about me, princess?"

She hit my arm again. "They're not *naughty* dreams."

"So, you admit it was about me." I grinned. "Wait. Dream*s* as in plural? You've dreamt about me more than once?"

"Ugh," she groaned, putting her tomato-red face back in her hands. "Of course, that's what you picked out of that sentence."

I made a show of brushing off my shoulders and adjusting the collar of my shirt. "Feel free to keep having those dreams if it means you kissing me some more."

Maya rolled her eyes, but I could see the smile she was fighting. "Don't let it go to your head too much, Oliver. They're just dreams."

I nodded, pressing my lips together. "Keep telling yourself that, princess. But please, feel free to keep falling asleep in my arms." I gave her a wink that awarded me a light punch to the arm. I enjoyed making this woman flustered, way more than I should.

An easy quiet fell in the car. Maya blinked, likely remembering why we were in the car to begin with.

"Did it stop snowing?"

"It appears so. I'll go check." I slipped my feet back into my boots and pulled the knit cap over my head before climbing out of the Jeep, stifling a groan as my legs fully extended for the first time in hours.

The world was a literal winter wonderland. At least a foot of snow had fallen while we were asleep. The car was covered, but it wasn't buried enough to where we wouldn't be able to pull back on the road. It still looked treacherous, but at least the wind wasn't whipping the snow around anymore. Daylight was fading fast, and I would rather risk the roads while there was still some light than try it in the dark.

I grabbed the ice scraper from the trunk and used the brush end to swipe the snow off the Jeep. A few minutes later, the snow was on the ground, and I was back in the front seat, turning the blessed heat on in the car.

"What's the verdict?" Maya asked as I rubbed my hands together to warm them up.

"We'll have to go slow, but it's better now than it was."

With a nod, she crawled back into the front seat, buckled her seatbelt, and switched her phone on as I pulled back onto the main road.

"Holy poop!" she said as she looked at her phone. "It's after three!"

I laughed. Somehow, such a phrase fit her perfectly.

"We slept for almost five hours."

"Best nap of my life," I said in answer, earning me another snort.

It was slow going as we drove through the country roads toward Meridel. Maya was quiet for much of the drive, which left me in spinning thoughts over our kiss, wondering how I could get it to happen again.

We were thirty minutes from Meridel when my phone rang, coming through the Bluetooth in my car again. This time I checked before answering. My father. Of course.

"Are you going to answer that?" Maya asked as it continued to ring.

"I think I'll pass." My father never had anything good to say, and the last thing I wanted was for him to burst the perfect Maya bubble my head was living in after that kiss.

"You should answer it, Oliver. Just pretend I'm not here."

I grunted and said quietly, "Not likely," then forced a breath into my lungs and hit the answer button on the steering wheel.

"Hello?"

"Oliver? Where have you been?" As usual, his tone was demanding which had my insides clenching tight.

My finger twitched to hit the end call button. *Already off to a great start.*

"Driving. Didn't have a signal."

He *harrumphed*. "Well, this is important."

"I'm waiting."

I swear I could hear him roll his eyes.

"I received a phone call from my assistant. There's

a couple not far from Meridel that had inquired about having an engagement session done after seeing your photos in that magazine. They want to utilize the fresh snowfall and do it tomorrow while everything is white. I need you to do it."

"That's very last minute."

"They offered to pay double the usual rate."

My mouth flopped open. My father's company already had a reputation for being expensive, but double? As nice as the money would be, I wasn't interested if it took me away from my time with Maya.

"I told you I was on an indefinite break," I said.

"Exactly. Then you'll have nothing better to do."

"A break means no photography."

"Then do it as a favor to your father."

"And why do you think you deserve a favor?"

I saw Maya cringe out of the corner of my eye.

"I need you to do this shoot for me, Son. I'm still in England for the next week, and you know we're still in the process of spreading our photographers into the States, never mind the fact that they specifically requested you."

I glanced at Maya, whose attention was on the snowy road in front of me. An idea bloomed in my mind, and I took a leap of faith.

"I'll do it under one condition."

My father sighed as if I had just asked him to climb a mountain and pick me a rare flower. "What is it?"

"I get to bring a second photographer, and she gets a cut of the money."

Maya tensed before turning those blue eyes on me.

"*She*?" my father asked. I couldn't tell if it was surprise or disdain in his voice. "These people are paying a lot of money and I don't need some girl messing everything up."

Fire burned in my belly. "For your information, that girl, *my girlfriend*, is a brilliant photographer who will only bring value to the shoot. That's my condition. Maya helps or I won't do it."

A beat of silence.

Maya's mouth was hanging open.

Mine might have been too.

I'd never spoken to my father like that before. I waited, expecting backlash and a scolding, but to my surprise he bit out, "Fine. I'll text you the details where to meet the couple."

And then he hung up.

I let out a long breath, wishing I wasn't driving so I could put my head between my knees and just *breathe*. My father always left me wound so tight I couldn't get air in my lungs and my muscles spasming from clenching them so hard.

"Oliver?" Maya asked with a hesitant voice. "Are you okay?"

Her voice was like slipping into a cold pool on a hot day, loosening all the tightly coiled pieces of me. Her hand reached over and covered mine, her thumb skimming the back of it.

"Yeah," I said, exhaling, her touch flooding me with peace. "I'm okay."

After a moment she asked, "Why did you do that?"

"It was the only way that I could bear the thought of doing this shoot for *him*."

She was quiet for a moment. "Why don't you two get along?"

I shook my head. "It's always been like that. He's always been harsh with me, pushing me to the very edge of my limits, then shoving me off just because he can. He loves to use me and my talent to further his own agenda." Maya's hand went still before she pulled away and I sighed, glancing over at her. She was fidgeting with her hands again. "That's part of why I came back to Meridel. I needed some distance to figure things out."

"Like what?"

My thumb beat against the steering wheel as I debated how much to tell her.

"He owns L.L. & Co, the photography agency I worked for back in London. I've been taking pictures for as long as I can remember, and he's never missed an opportunity to exploit my talent. Now that I'm older, he's been wanting me to learn how to run the business so that when he retires, I can take over, but that's not the life I envisioned for myself."

Maya considered for a moment. "What do you envision for yourself then?"

I pursed my lips. That was the real question, and what I had come back to Meridel to figure out.

"I'm not sure yet, but I know it's not running my father's business. I love photography, and I'm good at it, but when it's tied to him it taints everything. I want to become successful because of my ability, not my connections. I don't want to be exploited for someone else's gain anymore.

"I want my photos to mean something. I want to do things that bring me joy instead of what's necessary for a paycheck. Maybe someday I'll have my own photography business. I don't know. I just know that his plan for my life isn't what I want."

Maya nodded, biting her lip, and offering reassurance in the silent way only she could.

"So, you'll help with the photoshoot?"

Her thumbs twiddled in her lap before she gave me a crooked smile. "I think I can make it happen."

I grabbed her hand and kissed it. "Thank you, Maya."

The tiny sign that told us we were entering Meridel appeared a while later. Night had descended, and the streets were devoid of all signs of life. Everyone had hunkered down for the storm, and Main Street was dark except for the string lights between the buildings.

Everything was closed, and not a single car lined the road.

"I was going to get dinner for you before I took

you home, but it looks like everything is closed," I said, stomach sinking. My romantic plan for the day had been ruined by the snow.

At least you got an epic kiss out of it.

"That's okay. I think I have some ramen in the pantry."

Ugh. Just stick a knife in my heart.

"Ramen?"

She nodded. "It's a delicacy for broke people in America."

I winced, hating the mental image of Maya curled up with a bowl of noodles by herself. "Sorry, but you're not eating ramen tonight."

Maya laughed. "I hate to break it to you, but I don't have another choice."

"Yes, you do."

She cocked her head. "Oh? Do tell."

I gave her a smug look that made her gulp. "You're coming to my place. I'll cook you something better than *ramen.*"

Maya

I kissed Oliver Lewis.

I wasn't one for cursing, I preferred to make up outlandish, goofy sayings instead, but I had a whole line of expletives that I was screaming at myself inside my head. What was I thinking?

That kiss never should have happened.

But even worse, I had the niggling desire to do it again.

Maya, what the heck is wrong with you?

And, to top it off, Oliver shared that his dad had a habit of using him to get ahead, and that made me feel like the most horrible person because wasn't that exactly what I was doing? *Using* Oliver to get to his dad and win the contest? My stomach twisted into knots.

And, like an idiot, I agreed to help him with that

engagement shoot tomorrow. He was risking a lot for me by making his father agree to this. What if my photos weren't any good? What if I let him down?

Countless more what-ifs floated through my mind, pummeling at my insides until every ounce of confidence I had in my skills was cracked, and only insecurity and doubt remained.

And to make matters *even worse*, I was in Oliver's townhouse, sitting on his couch, breathing in the scent of sandalwood and something smoky, like incense, that lingered in the air. The tree he picked out was leaning against the wall, still bundled in red string, and dripping melted snow onto the floor. There were a few decorations here and there, but it didn't feel like Christmas was being shoved down my throat.

I glanced over my shoulder to where Oliver was cooking dinner in the kitchen. I should have been nice and offered to help, but at the moment, I couldn't be anywhere near him. Since my need to hate him and my desire to kiss him again were at war with each other, I couldn't be held accountable for whatever happened if I put myself near him.

But I couldn't deny that Oliver had a way of bringing out a side of me that I didn't usually let see the light of day. He saw the loud pieces that I let everyone see, but he also saw the anxious and hesitant parts I desperately tried to keep hidden—the things that might drive people to leave.

But Oliver wasn't frightened by those fragile pieces of me. And, if I was honest, I didn't hate that I was able to be myself around him—anxiety and all.

I massaged my forehead, the memory of the kiss replaying in my mind over and over. If I hadn't had that stupid dream, I never would have *ever* dared to kiss Oliver.

The dream flashed through my head and my face burst into flames.

Ugh.

Of course, I would have a dream about him while we were stranded in his car, sharing a blanket, and cuddling to stay warm. I smacked my forehead repeatedly.

So stupid, Maya.

"Everything okay?" Oliver asked, making me jump.

I looked over my shoulder to find him leaning in the doorway to the kitchen, wiping his hands with a towel, a giant smirk on his face.

Like the couch had become a trampoline, I sprang to my feet and started fluffing cushions that absolutely did not need it. Oliver's long dark-gray couch was the most comfortable thing I'd ever sat on, the fabric soft as a baby's butt and the cushions plump yet squishy.

Really, Maya? His couch is like a plump baby's butt?

Oliver watched me smacking and punching the pillows, the corners of his mouth twitching, probably to keep from laughing at my ridiculous display.

"What are you doing?" he asked after a few more moments of my insanity.

"Oh, err, nothing!" All the words had escaped from my brain, and only gibberish was left.

It was just a kiss, Maya! Why are you acting like a complete fool?

My body was full of anxious energy, and I had to keep moving. After I had smacked the crap out of the couch, I moved on to straightening the small stack of books that was laying on the coffee table—even though they were straight already—banging my knee in the process.

Oliver was going to think I'd lost my mind.

I bent down, looking at the books from every angle to make sure each corner was aligned, ignoring the ache in my knee. Warm hands circled my arms, pulling me upright.

"Maya?" Oliver asked as he turned me to face him, a strange mix of amusement and concern flickering in his eyes. "What's the matter?"

I shook my head. I couldn't tell Oliver that I was unable to stop thinking about our kiss in his Jeep—or how much I wanted to do it again. He'd never let me live it down and would tease me endlessly for the rest of the time he was forced to be my chauffeur.

"Nothing's wrong," I said through a fake smile. Oliver didn't look convinced.

"Hmm, well, as convincing as that was," he said, backing away and heading into the kitchen. "Dinner is ready if you're hungry."

The words *hungry for your kisses* sat on the tip of my

tongue, and I bit down hard to keep them at bay, nodding with a closed lip smile. I followed him into the kitchen where the smell of meat and potatoes engulfed me.

A small groan escaped through my lips at the glorious aroma, and Oliver quirked an eyebrow. My cheeks burned beneath his gaze.

He dished out mashed potatoes on a plate before plopping sausages on top. Then he poured two glasses of rosé and led me into the little dining room. A small square table sat against the wall, one chair on each side. A long red candle with a dancing flame sat in the middle, a loaf of bread next to it. He set our plates down and I followed with the glasses before we each took a seat.

My stomach gurgled again as I tried not to drool over my food.

"This looks good," I said, trying to maintain nonchalance. It might have been as simple as meat and potatoes, but it smelled divine, and I briefly entertained the idea of sticking my face into it like a child.

"Better than ramen?"

I picked up my fork and scooped up a bite of potatoes. "That's yet to be determined."

Oliver's smirk had my ears turning to little flames as I popped it in my mouth.

The first bite was stupid good. So good that I almost got up and did a little cheerleading cheer.

"Definitely better than ramen," I murmured, hating to admit that my archnemesis was right about the food, and that he was also a very good cook.

Blasted Brit.

I didn't miss Oliver's pleased smile before he dug into his own food.

After too many moments of chewing in silence, I blurted, "Why did you come back to Meridel?" in typical blunt Maya fashion.

He hesitated for a brief second, his fork frozen in the air, before he popped a bite into his mouth. Was he avoiding my question?

Finally, he swallowed and said, "I prefer Meridel over England."

I blinked at him. "How could you like this tiny town better than *England?*"

He gave the smallest shake of his head. "London is busy and loud and it's too easy to feel insignificant and lost. At least here, people know your name, give you a smile, and wave as you pass by on the street. It's easier to feel like *somebody* here instead of just another number in a crowded city."

His words resonated so strongly within me that they stole the breath from my lungs.

"I also much prefer the company of those in Meridel," he added with a wink.

Did he mean *me?*

I scrunched my nose. "Why would you enjoy the nosiness of this small town over the invisibility that a big city affords you?"

Oliver shook his head. "Invisibility is overrated."

"Why?"

"Imagine living in a place with thousands upon thousands of people, all completely enamored with their own lives. When you walk through the city and pass people, they just look *through* you instead of *at* you. They don't care at all what you're going through—whether you're on top of the world or at the end of your rope. You could live day-to-day with no interaction with people—no sign that anyone cares or values your existence."

His words made my heart ache. Was that how he truly felt? Underneath that cocky, tough exterior, was Oliver Lewis just wanting to be seen and valued? To feel like he mattered to someone?

The thought cracked straight through my deteriorating hatred of him.

Maybe we were more alike than I ever imagined.

I took a sip of wine. "But your family is in England."

An unamused laugh puffed from his lips, and he took a sip of his own. "My mum is from Iowa and was quite young when she married my father. They lived in England for most of my life, but a few years ago, she started spending half the year here to see her family more often. My father, being the type of person he is, had no qualms about it. He travels back and forth every few months, but primarily stays in England."

"That sounds miserable." The words were out of my

mouth before I could filter them. I couldn't imagine being married to someone, only to spend half the year away from them and be *okay* with it.

Oliver shrugged. "My father is not the easiest person to be around, so I don't really blame my mum for wanting to be here more often. That's why I came to Meridel last year in the first place—to visit her. I didn't expect to fall in love…"

He trailed off and every nerve within me prickled. He coughed and quickly added, "with the town. I fell in love with the *town*." Oliver cleared his throat. "It's charming and I quite enjoy it."

I swallowed hard. "Right, of course. The town."

A blush colored his cheeks and he seemed to be scrambling to come up with something to say.

"Um, tell me something about you," he tried before sipping his drink.

I cocked my head. "You think you've earned my secrets, Brit?"

One of his shoulders lifted in a partial shrug. "I'm doing my best, Maya."

The breath whooshed out of my lungs at his honesty. He *did* seem to be trying to earn my trust. As much as I always thought he was a bad guy, he hadn't given me many reasons to continue thinking that way—even if I hated to admit it.

I thought for a moment, struggling to come up with something to share with him without being *too* vulnerable.

"The photoshoot I did with Elsie and Jameson… that was the first time I ever felt like photography was something I could really do—something I could succeed at," I said. "It even inspired the name of my business, Sunflower Fields. I had worked so hard through that last semester of class, trying to improve my skills, and it all just seamlessly fit together by the time *The Heart Shot* came around." I paused, taking a breath, and staring at my plate.

"When I posted the photos on social media, it brought in an influx of inquiries, and for a while business was doing well. But then the emails stopped coming, and my posts no longer brought in clients, and it all felt… over."

I met his gaze. "Capturing the beauty of people in hidden ways that are so often overlooked and finding new ways to bring out peoples' inner light through pictures…it's all I want. I want them to find *their* happy when they look at the photos I take. Much like you, I want my photography to mean something. That's why…" I hesitated, unsure if I wanted to say the words that were begging to spill out of my mouth.

"That's why it felt like the end of the world when you won the class competition. That had been my big chance to make Sunflower Fields explode, but then…it slipped through my fingers just like that."

I hadn't meant to say *all* of that, but something about Oliver had the words falling off my lips.

Oliver's eyes softened, and he took my hand on the table, his thumb tracing a line across it. "I'm sorry, Maya. I didn't know how much it meant to you, and I never would've wanted to take that from you."

I tried to smile, words stalling on my tongue for once, but my lips wobbled. It was ridiculous that my eyes burned at his words. Such a simple statement shouldn't have such an effect, but for some reason, coming from Oliver, it meant so much more.

He had just started to lean forward, perhaps to kiss me, when my phone vibrated against my leg, and I flinched out of Oliver's touch. I was thankful for the distraction. He didn't need to see any more of my tears, and the thought of kissing him again made my emotions feel like they were on overload. With an apologetic smile, I fished out my phone from my pocket, ignoring the way he shifted in his seat and went back to eating.

ELSIE

Hey! Are you still in for tomorrow night? I haven't heard from you.

A weird sinking feeling settled into my stomach. Tomorrow night? What was she talking about?

ME

I'm scared to ask. What's tomorrow night?

ELSIE

You're kidding, right?

It's our Friendsmas!

Remember, you, me, and Jameson were going to have dinner together to celebrate Christmas before we go out of town? Did you forget?

Crap, I definitely forgot about that.

ME

That's tomorrow?

ELSIE

Yes, Maya, that's tomorrow.

Can you still come?

I glanced at Oliver. Was it too much to ask him to drive me to Jameson's house? As if hearing my thoughts, my phone buzzed with another text.

ELSIE

You should bring Oliver! The more the merrier ;)

ME

I'm not sure that's a great idea, Els.

ELSIE

And why not, Maya? Give me one good reason.

A moment passed with my brain unable to think of a single excuse for why I wouldn't want Oliver to come to Friendsmas. Because, if I were honest with myself, I *did* want him to come.

But that was a dangerous thought that I couldn't let myself entertain.

Another text popped onto the screen.

ELSIE

Consider it another chance to practice before the real dinner with his family!

Well, when she put it that way...

ME

Fine, I'll ask him.

ELSIE

Great! See you both tomorrow at seven!

I exhaled a long breath as I locked my phone and slid it back in my pocket.

"Everything okay?" Oliver's voice tore me from my thoughts.

"Hmm? Oh, yeah. Um..." I wasn't sure how to ask my fake boyfriend to come to Friendsmas. And why was there a part of me that was scared he'd say no?

Ugh. I was doing a terrible job of viewing him as the

enemy and thinking of him far too much in…non-enemy ways. Flashes of our kiss in the Jeep went through my mind and my stomach fluttered, forcing me to duck my head.

In one smooth motion, Oliver moved his chair so it was next to me, and a warm finger appeared under my chin, tilting my face up to meet those blue eyes that I swore saw right through me.

"Maya?"

"Um…"

He leaned closer, his eyes flicking to my lips.

He was going to kiss me.

I needed to pull away, stop him.

But why didn't I *want* to stop him?

Why was *I* leaning forward too?

Just as his breath tickled my lips, I blurted, "Friendsmas!" and sprang to my feet, stumbling over the leg of his chair.

Oliver's hands grabbed onto my hips to keep me from face-planting onto the floor, and then he cocked his head at me. "Pardon?"

I stepped out of his grip, the distance between us allowing me to gulp down a breath. "Tomorrow night is Friendsmas."

"What is Friendsmas?" The way he sounded the word out in his accent was adorable.

Dang it, no it wasn't! Oliver is not adorable!

I bit my lip to hold back my chuckle, and his eyes

tracked the movement.

"Usually, I spend Christmas with either Elsie or Jameson and his mom, but they're going out of town this year. So, instead, we're having dinner tomorrow night to celebrate before they leave. Elsie, um, said that you're invited."

His eyes widened before that smug smile graced his lips.

"But only so we can practice!" I reminded him as he stood and took a step toward me. I couldn't let him think he was invited because of any other reason.

There is *no other reason, Maya.*

"Of course. Purely for practicing our fake relationship." He stepped closer. "What a grand idea." Another step.

My heart pounded in my chest. "Do we really need the practice though?"

Oliver's hand went to my hip, tugging me closer so that our chests were nearly touching.

"I'll take any excuse I can get to be with you." He paused to brush my hair behind one ear, his fingertips skimming the lightest trail across my cheek. "—to see you. To touch you—"

Then his lips crushed mine.

This kiss was different from the one we shared in the Jeep.

That one was impulsive, brought on by that ridiculous dream, but this one was all fire.

There was no hesitation as he tilted my head, deepening the kiss. Oliver's hands were like a brand on my skin, burning every inch of me. His grip was strong yet gentle, as if this moment was the most important thing to him. The way he held me was almost...reverent.

Yet it didn't dim the heat and passion flaring between us.

For over a year I had hated Oliver Lewis with every fiber of my being.

So why did kissing him now feel so *right?*

And why didn't I want to stop?

Step by step, Oliver backed me toward the wall, never breaking contact, until every inch of him pressed against me. My fingers pressed into his neck and tangled into his hair, his hands moving from my waist to cup my face. I felt like the most important thing in the world to him, and after growing up with a childhood like mine, being important to someone was everything.

I could get used to this.

Those words repeated in my head over and over as I kissed Oliver, relishing the feel of his skin under my fingers, the way his hands pressed into me.

Wait! Oliver is the enemy! Do I need to remind you that he stole your chances at a future in photography when he won that spread in the Iowa Artist Gazette? *Or that you're just using him to get to his dad?*

The thoughts were a bucket of cold water splashed on my head and I pulled back, breaking the kiss. Oliver breathed heavily as he rested his forehead against mine. He probably thought I pulled away to slow us down, but it was actually because I was freaking out, trying to remember why all of this was a terrible idea.

As much as my body wanted Oliver, and even despite my confession and his apology, I had to remember what he had done to me—and what I planned to do to him to move forward with my life.

Oliver was merely a means to an end. After Christmas was over, I wouldn't have to see him again. Hopefully I will have won the photo contest, and be on my way to paying off my debt and finally looking toward the future for once.

A less stressful life with a promising future career and no debt was within my grasp, I couldn't afford to let Oliver distract me from it.

He brushed my hair behind an ear and was starting to lean in for another kiss when I pulled out of his embrace and smoothed down my shirt. "I'm sorry, Oliver. I should get home. It's getting late."

Something flickered over his face, too fast to decipher, and I felt it like a knife to my gut. For the first time since I had met Oliver Lewis, I didn't want to hurt him. What did that say about me and my feelings?

He moved back, giving me space. "Right. Of course. Let me clean up dinner and I'll drive you home."

I nodded, unable to meet his eyes.

Why did I feel so horrible when this was the right thing to do for me and my future? Keeping distance between us was for the best, so why couldn't I convince my heart of that?

A few minutes later, the table was cleared, and we

donned our coats and boots before climbing back into his Jeep. It was far too silent as he drove me to my apartment. I didn't know what to say to ease the strange tension that had settled between us, and part of me figured I shouldn't even try.

Our relationship was fake, and that's how it needed to stay.

Oliver pulled up next to my building, and I wished I could hear what he was thinking if only to know that I hadn't hurt him too much.

But then again, why did I suddenly care about hurting him? This is why I needed to put distance between us. I couldn't develop feelings and use him at the same time.

With a sigh, I slid out of the Jeep. "Thanks again for dinner, Oliver."

"Anytime." His voice was hesitant. "I'll pick you up in the morning?"

I froze. "In the morning?"

"The engagement shoot?"

Crap on a stick.

In the chaos of that mind-blowing kiss, I had completely forgotten about it. A shoot in the morning and then Friendsmas in the evening?

Double crap on a stick.

"Oh. Right. Yeah."

A strange emotion flashed through Oliver's eyes, and he gave a nod before I closed the door, pausing once I got inside to watch as he pulled away from the curb and onto the street. I didn't know how long I stood there staring through the cold glass, but Oliver's Jeep was long gone by the time I went up to my apartment.

I let out a long, shuddering breath.

Friendsmas with Oliver Lewis.

This'll be so fun.

Oliver

I was confused.

One moment, Maya was into the kiss as much as I was, and the next she was pulling away, putting far too much space between us. Something had changed in a split second, and I had no idea what.

Kissing her was everything. It was wild, electric, and my new favorite past time. I wanted to spend forever doing it.

It was a dangerous thought—wanting to spend forever with Maya Beck.

Especially since she was still adamant that she hated me, and now she'd slammed on the brakes when I thought we were finally getting somewhere.

She tried to fight it, a valiant effort, but she felt *some-*

thing for me. She wouldn't kiss me like *that* if she didn't. What I didn't know was to what extent her feelings were, and if she'd be able to get over whatever was holding her back so that we could give this a proper go.

Because if there was one thing I was certain about, it was that I needed this fake relationship to be real.

I tossed and turned all night long, my mind racing over the last twenty-four hours. By the time light started peeking through the curtains it had felt like the longest night of my life, and I rubbed my eyes, trying to force the tiredness away.

I rolled out of bed, my feet slapping against the wood floor as I looked out the window. The sun was beginning to poke its head over the horizon, glistening off the fresh snow, but clouds were rolling in. Good, that would make the photoshoot a little easier, and give it that true winter feel.

I checked the watch on my nightstand. It was barely even seven in the morning. I had hours before the photo-shoot.

Since I was technically on break from work, there was nothing pressing that I needed to get done, and yet it didn't stop my heart from racing, my mind from spinning. With no other way to calm my mind, I threw on some shorts and headed downstairs to work out.

It wasn't my favorite thing in the world, but it always helped center me; helped chase away the demons holding my heart and mind hostage, at least for a little while, so it was worth the time and effort. An hour of weightlifting and cardio later, my chest was a little looser, my mind a little more focused.

After showering, making breakfast, and getting everything packed for the photoshoot, I headed out to my Jeep. We were supposed to meet the couple thirty minutes outside of Meridel, which gave me enough time to grab some coffee, pick up Maya, and drive out there.

I shot a text to Maya, letting her know I was on my way. I couldn't help smiling a little at the name I gave her.

ME

Good morning, princess. I hope you slept well. I'll be on my way to pick you up soon. Would you like coffee from The Roasted Bean?

I was halfway to the coffee shop before a response appeared.

PRINCESS MAYA

It should be illegal to be up this early.

[GIF of a tired child]

I laughed.

ME

You know it's after nine in the morning, right?

PRINCESS MAYA

Mornings are of the devil.

ME

Then allow me to make it easier.

What's your drink of choice?

I pulled into a spot on the side of the street, struggling to get out of my Jeep with the mounds of snow on the sidewalk from the snowstorm yesterday, and headed into the coffee shop. My phone vibrated a moment later.

PRINCESS MAYA

A cold brew with two pumps of vanilla and a splash of cream.

Please.

With a smile, I ordered her cold brew and a latte for myself, and ten minutes later Maya was crawling into my car, camera bag on her shoulder. Her blonde hair was piled in a messy bun, and she was decked out in poofy black snow gear like we were going on a skiing trip instead. Her giant coat swallowed her small frame. I flicked on her seat warmer and turned up the heat to counteract the cold that had burst into the car when Maya got inside.

I handed her the cold brew she requested.

"Thanks," she said, giving the drink the biggest heart

eyes I'd ever seen. My next goal was to get her to look at *me* like that.

"Ready for today?" I asked, pulling away from her apartment building and heading to the park where we were meeting the couple. The roads were still slippery—the snowplows hadn't made it onto the country roads yet—but it was still leagues better than driving back from the tree farm.

Maya snuggled her camera bag against her chest. "Born ready." Her words were certain, but the way she bit her lip made me wonder if she was nervous. I didn't want her nervous—I wanted her to feel confident.

"So, I was thinking that you could take the lead today," I said, keeping my voice as calm as possible. This was either a brilliant plan I had come up with in the wee hours of the morning, or it would backfire and slap me in the face.

She choked on her coffee, dabbing drops of liquid from her chin. "Excuse me?"

"I want you to run the photoshoot as if it were your own."

She gaped at me. "Why?"

"Because I know you can do it."

Maya gave me a skeptical look. "I don't think your dad will like that."

"What he doesn't know won't hurt him. I'll still be there, I just won't be running the show."

"Why would you want me to do this?"

I smiled and her cheeks turned pink. "Because you're an excellent photographer, and you deserve a chance to show off. I want to see that spark in you again—the one you had when you presented your stranger shoot pictures. I want you to remember why you love this so much. Besides, I have no doubt you'll do a great job."

Though she'd never said it in any certain terms, I had a feeling that ever since I won the community college competition, she had been doubting her ability with a camera. Truthfully, I don't know why I won instead of her. Her photos were just as good if not better than mine. Maya was too talented to believe that she was subpar. If letting her run this photoshoot helped remind her of both her skill and passion, then I was happy to do it—and face whatever wrath my father meted out.

Maya's eyes brightened, her whole face lighting up. "Are you sure?"

The look on her face alone made it more than worth it.

"Positive, Maya. For two hours, you can boss me around to your heart's content."

She cocked her head, a devious smile spreading across her face. "Careful what you wish for, Oliver."

I smiled back. "Do your worst, princess. Do you worst."

Maya was brilliant.

That was the only way to describe her as she photographed the couple. From the moment we stepped out of the car and introduced ourselves to Garrett and Trina, the soon-to-be Lofsons, a switch flipped, and a new side of Maya came out that I hadn't seen before.

It was more than confidence that filled each of Maya's movements or the way she instructed the couple. It was pure joy. There wasn't an ounce of hesitation in her body language, in the way she spoke to Garrett and Trina, or in the chorus of clicking coming from her camera.

Maya was a natural when it came to photography, that much was clear. Just when I thought she'd run out of poses or needed a helpful hint of what to do next, she surprised me and remained a step ahead the entire time, even joking with them from time to time.

The couple caught on to her vivacious energy, completely at ease as they held each other in their arms, even when Maya made them spread out in the snow and make snow angels side by side.

For a moment, I worried that the Lofsons would hate getting down into the cold, wet snow, but to my utter shock, not only did they love it, they ended up laughing and having a snowball fight, Maya's camera going the entire time.

Even *I* couldn't help snapping a few pictures myself. Not that Maya would need them. Maya knew what she was doing with a camera, that much was clear. Even though she talked a big game about bossing me around, Maya had barely told me to do anything. Not that I was complaining. It allowed me to watch her work, to see the way she lit up behind the camera, all her insecurities disappearing. It was beautiful.

Maya had her spark back and it took my breath away.

It had been a little over an hour and my feet were numb in my boots, but the cold didn't seem to bother Maya at all.

"Okay, let's have you two stand over there in front of those trees," Maya instructed, pulling me from my thoughts. "Mr. Lofson, I want you to dip your bride backward as if you were dancing and hold her there." The couple eagerly complied, and as they held the pose, the love they felt for one another gleamed in their eyes.

Maya's camera continued clicking as she looked over her shoulder at me and gave me a smile that had my heart stuttering in my chest. It was a look that told me she was having the time of her life.

I'd do anything to bring that smile to her face every single day.

A hopeful vision of the future flashed through my mind—one of us running a photography business together. I wasn't sure Maya would ever entertain such a notion, but the desire to make it happen was like a slow burning fire, consuming me from the inside out.

I gave her a reassuring nod and she returned her attention to the couple, giving a few last poses to try before we wrapped up for the day. Unable to help myself, I peeked over Maya's shoulder to get a glimpse of the photos she was taking, and a swell of warmth filled my entire body. They were *beautiful*, well worth what the couple had paid.

"Thank you again for doing this so last minute," Garrett remarked as Maya finished packing up her camera.

"Yes, this has been a dream!" Trina said, her eyes bright with excitement.

"Anytime," Maya and I said in unison which caused us all to chuckle.

Trina gave us a knowing look. "How long have you two been together?"

Maya tripped over the flat snow at the question, fidgeting with the strap of her bag. "Oh, um—"

"It's still new," I supplied, putting an arm around Maya's shoulders, and Trina smiled in understanding. Maya's body was stiff, her eyes fixed on the ground in front of her. I wished I could read her mind to know what she was thinking.

"We'll get the photos to you as soon as possible," I said, trying to change the subject so that Maya would loosen up again.

Garrett and Trina hugged both of us, much to my surprise, and thanked us once more before leaving the park.

Silence settled between me and Maya, the cold biting at my numb fingers and toes, but I ignored it. We stood outside the Jeep, watching as the couple drove away. When they were out of sight, I turned to her with a grin on my face.

"That was incredible, princess. You have a gift."

Maya's ears reddened. "It's been so long...I forgot how much I love this." Her eyes met mine. "Thank you for letting me do this, Oliver."

I took her hand and raised it to my lips. "Anything for you, darling."

Thanks to the remote start on my Jeep, the cab was nice and warm as I opened the door for Maya and waited for her to crawl inside. A moment later we headed back to Meridel. I felt like I had gulped down seven cold brews. I was on a high from watching the girl I'm crazy about do what she loved.

"Do you mind if I handle the editing?" Maya asked, breaking me from my thoughts. I glanced at her. She was wringing her hands in her lap again.

"Of course. I wouldn't have it any other way, Maya." I wouldn't dream of trying to edit her photos—not when they were hers to begin with.

A relieved smile curled her lips as she settled farther into her seat.

"Did you want lunch before I take you home?" *Please spend more time with me. I hate saying goodbye to you.*

Maya shook her head. "No, I think I'll try to nap and then get started editing those photos before Friendsmas tonight."

My stomach sank but I fought to keep my expression neutral as I nodded. I wasn't ready to part ways or take her back home yet. I would have loved to spend the rest of the day together, but I didn't want to interrupt this new life that had sparked within her. So, thirty minutes later, with a promise to pick her up before dinner, I dropped her off at home and then proceeded to sit at my house for hours.

I tried to nap, but every time I closed my eyes, all I saw was Maya smiling behind the camera. I had hoped getting out of the house might help, so I drove back to Main Street, but when I ended up in a little gift shop, everything inside reminded me of her. I hurried back home after that.

I thought I had had it bad for her before, but it was nothing compared to how I felt after just a couple weeks of being her chauffeur and getting to know her. I was relieved when it was time to get dressed and leave the house.

There was a strange prickling feeling in my stomach as I drove to pick her up. Was I...nervous?

What was there to be nervous about? I had already met Elsie and Jameson. This would be an easy evening with food and friends. There was nothing to worry about. So why did I feel like this?

I glanced in the rearview mirror at the small, gift-wrapped package in the backseat. I wasn't certain whether they'd be exchanging gifts tonight or not, but I brought something for Maya, just in case. I didn't expect anything in return, but when I saw it in the shop earlier, I couldn't resist buying it for her.

Pulling up next to her apartment building, I shifted into park and waited, my thumbs drumming against the steering wheel. Usually Maya was waiting outside, so I found it strange that she was nowhere to be found.

ME

I'm outside whenever you're ready.

The three bouncing dots appeared almost immediately.

PRINCESS MAYA

Maybe you should go without me.

What?

ME

They're YOUR friends. Why would I go without you?

PRINCESS MAYA

I don't think I can go.

My stomach sank. As nervous as I was, I had been looking forward to *practicing* some more.

ME

Are you okay?

It took a few seconds for a response to appear.

PRINCESS MAYA

I'm stuck.

ME

Pardon?

A moment later my phone rang. It was so loud in the silence of my Jeep that I jumped.

A frustrated exhale on the other end made the line crackle as I accepted the call. "Oliver?"

"Why, hello, princess. How are you?"

She grunted. "My dress is stuck."

Of all the things I expected her to say, I didn't expect her to say *that*.

"Oh. That's rather unfortunate. Uh…"

"The zipper got stuck, I can't reach it, and now I can't get it off." Her voice sounded utterly defeated.

"Um," I said, my brain stuttering over the mental image of Maya in a dress.

"Oliver, I need your help," she said. There was a slight wobble in her voice, and the sound of it threatened to undo me.

"I'll be right there." She sighed before I ended the

call and jumped out of the car.

Snow was starting to fall, drifting in lazy circles from the sky. I buzzed her apartment on the intercom and waited for the door to unlock before jogging up the stairs and down the hall.

I had just raised my hand to knock when the door opened, revealing Maya's dejected face. Her blonde hair was curled in loose waves, her makeup subtle aside from bright red lips that were perfectly kissable. The breath caught in my throat when I saw the dress she was wearing, though not for the reason it should have.

Maya looked like she was wearing tinsel from a Christmas tree. Were those...sequins? It did incredible things for her figure but looked...itchy.

"I know. It's hideous," Maya admitted, interpreting my expression the wrong way. She waved me inside.

"Hideous is not quite the word I would have used," I said, following her, careful to keep my gaze from the open zipper that exposed half of her back.

She led me down a short hallway into her bedroom where her pink floral bedspread was covered with clothes. The room smelled like her—pears mixed with some sort of flower.

The walls were covered in framed photographs, all of them likely hers. There was a large dresser on one wall with a mirror next to it, and a small shelf on the other side of the room that held various knickknacks. I stepped closer to get a better look when I noticed a colorful piece of paper sticking off the shelf.

It was a flyer for the *Rising Star Photography Contest*.

Why—how—did she have that?

Had she entered the contest too? If she had, why wouldn't she have told me?

"What word would you use then?" she asked, spinning to face me, and cutting my perusal of her room—and my thoughts about the contest—short. "Ugly? Disastrous? Unflattering?"

Pushing the contest out of my mind, I reached out a hand, wrapping my fingers around her arm. Maya stilled, glancing down at where I touched her before meeting my gaze. Her blue eyes filled my entire body with a flood of heat.

"None of those, princess. You look beautiful. It just…looks uncomfortable."

She snorted. "You have no idea."

"Then why wear it?"

"It's called trying to be pretty."

"But you don't need to *try*."

Maya cocked her head, blinking at me like I had spoken another language. I stepped closer.

"You always look beautiful. There is no trying. You're effortlessly pretty, darling."

She continued staring at me, as if my words were gibberish. I needed her to understand how I saw her. I laid my hands on her shoulders and guided her over to the mirror.

"Tell me what you see," I told her.

Maya rolled her eyes. "Oliver, what's the point—"

"Tell me what you see, princess."

She sighed, her body tensing beneath my hands still resting on her shoulders.

"I see…dark circles under my eyes, and the heavy dose of concealer that I used to try to fix it. I see pale skin and dry, stringy hair, and too much extra fat on my body that I can't bring myself to do anything about."

She poked at her hips as if that's where the offending fat was, but I had no idea what she was talking about. Sure, she had curves, but no one would ever dare to call Maya fat. Besides, I thought her body was perfect the way it was.

"I see…" A heavy exhale escaped her lips. "I see someone who's tired of trying so hard for things to change and then being disappointed when it all falls apart."

Maya's eyes glistened and she bit her bottom lip. I waited for her to go on, but her chin trembled. I hated that that was all she saw in herself.

I brushed the hair over her shoulder, letting my fingers linger on her skin, bending so my lips brushed her ear, and stepped close until my chest was flush with her back. I met her eyes in the mirror.

"That's not what I see. I see a perfectly imperfect woman who tries her absolute best, who's an incredible friend, and who works her butt off every single day. I see a woman who has experienced awful things that no human should have to go through, and yet she's risen above all the struggle and become an amazing person despite it.

"I see a woman with stunning blue eyes that squeeze the breath from my lungs, and a gorgeous body that makes it a struggle to keep my hands to myself when all I want to do is hold her. I see a kind, gentle person that goes after what she wants, but doesn't step on people to get there."

I had to bite down on my tongue to keep from adding, *I see a woman that I'm desperately in love with.*

Tears filled her eyes as she looked at me in the mirror. "You see all of that?"

"And so much more."

Maya turned to face me, and I cupped her face with my hands, my thumbs brushing away the tears that escaped. I pressed my lips to her forehead.

"You're stunning, Maya. Inside and out." The words were whisper soft.

Her nose nudged mine once, twice, before her lips brushed against mine. They tasted like salty tears and chocolate.

As much as I wanted to lose myself in the kiss, I let her lead. I didn't want to take advantage of her frazzled state. Besides, we still had dinner to get to. After another gentle kiss, she pulled back, swiping her eyes.

"Sorry." Her cheeks flushed.

"You don't need to apologize, princess." The words *I love you* almost slipped out again and I fought the urge to kick myself. I really needed to get a grip.

This wasn't the time or place for that type of admission.

Maya didn't know that I had liked her for over a year; that everything I learned about her, every moment spent with her, only solidified what I had always sensed about her—what had drawn me to her in the first place.

She was an incredible person and I wanted to give her the world.

An "I love you" would seem sudden and crazy.

Maybe it *was* crazy.

"We should get going," she said, snapping me back to reality, her eyes widening as she looked at the time on her phone. "Can you…" She gestured at the zipper still halfway up her back.

"Oh. Yes." I stepped forward, my fingers brushing her back as I fought the stuck zipper. It took several tries, but it finally slid free. Trying to be a gentleman, I averted my eyes as it slid past her bra.

"Thanks," Maya said, holding the front of her dress. "I'll be out in a minute."

Recognizing that as a dismissal, I left her bedroom, closing the door behind me to give her privacy. A few minutes later, she emerged wearing a cream-colored sweater dress with leather leggings beneath. She looked warm and cozy and Christmassy. She was so beautiful it took my breath away.

"You look lovely, Maya."

A small smile curved her lips. "Thank you."

I helped her into her coat, and she grabbed a small bag of gifts from the kitchen counter before we headed back to my Jeep. The ride over to Jameson's house was quiet, but there was no tension or pressure to fill the silence.

Ten minutes later, I parked in the driveway, mentally preparing myself for whatever this night brought for Maya and me. We could call it pretending or faking all we wanted, but to me it was very, very real.

"Ready?" Maya asked, turning those blue eyes on me, stealing every ounce of air from my lungs.

I took hold of her hand, bringing the back of it to my lips, giving it a light kiss.

"With you, princess, I'm ready for anything."

Maya

With you, I'm ready for anything.

The words kept ping-ponging around in my mind as we made our way up the snowy walkway toward Jameson's house, my arm looped through Oliver's so I didn't slip.

The words themselves were simple, but I had learned that, with Oliver, nothing was simple, and I wondered what he meant by it.

After being convinced for so long that Oliver didn't like me and was out to get me, all these things he kept doing, like wanting to kiss me or looking at me in the mirror and pointing out all of the things *he* saw, it was getting harder and harder to still believe that. If anything, it seemed that he felt the opposite.

And where did that leave *my* feelings? Just yesterday I had resolved to continue hating him; to not let him distract me from my end goals. And yet, after what happened in my bedroom tonight, I didn't know if I could fight these growing feelings anymore.

What would happen if we...tried? What would happen if we agreed to stop faking a relationship and give a real one a shot? What if we stopped bluffing and admitted our feelings for each other?

The questions made my stomach swirl.

But then Elsie swung open the door with a huge smile and my thoughts came to a halt—or rather I shoved them into a box to examine later when I was alone.

"I'm so glad you guys came!" Elsie said, giving me a rib-breaking hug before giving Oliver an awkward side hug.

"Thank you for the invitation," Oliver replied. He had a small present in one of his hands. Was that...for me?

We stepped inside and shed our coats and shoes, Jameson's dog, Luna, bouncing around at our feet, waiting to be loved on. My senses were overwhelmed by the smell of ham and potatoes.

The Christmas decor was classy, and I suspected that it was thanks to Elsie more than Jameson. A frosted fake tree sat next to the fireplace, a few presents scattered underneath. Two stockings with each of their names hung from the mantle next to a mini one that had Luna's name on it. A scattering of tea light candles were snuggled in various places throughout the room making it feel cozy and romantic.

I went over to the tree and unloaded my bag of gifts, making sure to tuck Oliver's, which I made on a whim, in the very back, out of sight.

"Hey, Maya!" Jameson called from the kitchen before poking his head out of the doorway. "Welcome, Oliver."

We both nodded in acknowledgment and followed Elsie into the kitchen. I sighed. I loved Jameson's kitchen. With the light sage cabinets, black appliances, and gold hardware, it was a paradise in kitchen form. I didn't even like cooking that much, but if I had a kitchen like that, I could definitely learn to enjoy it.

"Make yourselves at home," Elsie said as she brought platters and glasses over to the table.

"Do you need any help?" Oliver asked.

She shook her head. "Nope. You two can have a seat on the couch and dinner will be ready in a few!" Elsie winked at me before disappearing back into the kitchen.

Oliver and I looked at each other awkwardly before we sunk down onto the couch. I kept a couple feet between us, and his hand twitched on the cushion behind me, as though it was annoyed that I wasn't within touching distance. Luna settled onto her giant bed in the corner, watching us. I swear her big brown eyes were telling me to scooch on over.

A moment later, Elsie's head popped out of the

kitchen, eyeing us. "That doesn't look very coupley." She pointed to the space between us.

I scowled at her, and she smiled.

With a roll of my eyes, I scooted down the couch, settling next to Oliver so that our hips were touching. His arm settled around my shoulders, pulling me closer.

"Better?" I snapped.

"Immensely," Elsie crooned before disappearing again.

I sighed. Did I enjoy sitting close to Oliver and having his arm around me? Yes, I did. But did my best friend have to look so gleeful about it?

No, she did not.

My body relaxed as his heat seeped into me, calming my nerves about tonight. Why I was nervous for a Christmas dinner with my best friend and cousin, I couldn't tell you, though I imagined it had something to do with the man currently running his fingers up and down my arm.

The doorbell rang and both of us flinched, jumping apart. He gave me a sheepish smile before pulling me back into him. Elsie hurried across the room, giving us a secretive grin, and my mouth fell open when she opened the door.

"Surprise!" Emma cried from the doorway, carrying a tote full of gifts in one hand and a duffle bag in the other.

"Emma?" I sprang to my feet and darted over to the door, throwing my arms around my cousin. "What are you doing here?" I pulled back to look at her. Her brown hair was pulled back in a french braid, her hazel eyes that matched Jameson's full of life.

"I'm here for Friendsmas, of course."

"I thought you were staying in the city for Christmas," I said, squeezing her again.

"I missed you all too much," she admitted, her eyes shimmering. "It's lonely in a big city without you guys. You can thank Elsie for orchestrating this."

We took turns hugging Emma before Jameson appeared a moment later and pushed me out of the way so he could pull his sister in for a tight hug.

Those two had been through so much over the years with their dad dying when they were young, and their mom fighting breast cancer. The struggle could have easily torn them apart, but they were closer than ever, even with Emma off at college.

"I'm so glad you came," he said, planting a kiss on the top of Emma's head.

She sniffled, smiling at her brother before shuffling her way inside.

Once Emma had set down her things and hung up her coat, she turned and found Oliver sitting on the couch. Her eyes went wide before giving me a *look*.

I scrambled for an explanation. "Oh, uh. This is Oliver."

The man in question stood to shake Emma's hand. "It's lovely to meet you."

"You too. And you are…"

Oliver said, "Maya's boyfriend," at the same time I

blurted, "Just a friend!"

Emma arched a brow, looking between us. "Well, which is it?"

I mentally kicked myself. Emma and I were usually super close, telling each other everything, but her college finals had taken over her life over the past couple of weeks. We barely had a chance to say hi to each other, let alone share what's going on in our lives. Otherwise, she would have already heard all about Oliver, this fake dating scheme, and the photography contest. I wished that Elsie had told me she was coming tonight. I would've made more of an effort to give Emma a heads-up.

Elsie laughed, throwing an arm around Emma's shoulders, and guiding her to the table. "Oh, we have a lot to catch you up on."

Jameson snorted. "I'll say."

Elsie clapped then. "Dinner is ready, everybody take a seat!"

Oliver and I made our way over to the table, sitting in the two seats by the wall as Elsie and Jameson brought out a giant platter of ham, followed by cheesy potatoes, rolls, a green bean casserole, and brown sugar smothered yams.

"Smells so good," Emma commented, putting her napkin on her lap.

Jameson handed Elsie a bottle of wine and she made quick work of filling our glasses.

Oliver's knee knocked mine under the table, but

instead of pulling away, he left it there, his heat flooding my leg.

"I know it's Christmas and not Thanksgiving," Jameson began once Elsie was seated, and he took her hand in his. "But this is the first holiday we've all been together like this. I'd love to start the meal with each of us saying one thing we're thankful for."

I expected there to be complaints, especially from Emma since she loved to eat almost as much as she loved severe weather, but to my surprise she sat there silent, a smile on her face.

"I'll go first," Elsie said. "I'm thankful for this handsome man next to me that I get to spend the rest of my life with, and for this table of friends, both old and new, making this life feel a lot less lonely."

The smile that Jameson gave her was brighter than the sun. "And I'm thankful for this beautiful woman I get to fall in love with a little more each day, and for family and friends that are healthy and *here*." He gave a meaningful look at Emma.

Emma smiled, her eyes glassy again. "I'm thankful for incredible people in my life who love me no matter what, no matter how far away I am." Jameson squeezed his sister's hand.

Everyone turned to Oliver next. His throat bobbed as he swallowed. "I am thankful for..." He hesitated before looking at me. "I'm thankful to have the chance to know this incredible woman beside me." His hand found my knee under the table. "To enjoy her company and find reasons to bring that beautiful smile to her face."

I swear I heard Emma and Elsie swooning.

I was trying not to swoon over his words.

My face heated as I looked around the table. I wasn't sure what to say. Of course, I was thankful for my cousins and Elsie. Each of them had played a role in walking me out of the dark times in my life.

All three of them had proven that there were people out there that wouldn't leave me—even if I still struggled to believe it sometimes. I didn't know where I'd be without Jameson's quiet, unconditional support, or Elsie's soft but fierce way of loving me, or Emma's protective nature. Though I still had healing and growing to do, I wouldn't be who I am—or maybe even *here*—without them.

I had so many things to be thankful for, but it was all too much to put into words.

And then there was Oliver. I was thankful for his belief in me, his kisses, and how I felt safe in his arms as he held me in his Jeep during the snowstorm. He made me feel loved and wanted even though I had tried to keep my walls up.

The more I thought about it, the more I realized Oliver reminded me of my friends. He supported me in both the big and small, quiet ways. He kept pulling me back to him, even when I was afraid of getting closer. Oliver pushed me to take steps of faith without throwing me to the wolves or allowing me to get hurt in the process.

And in that moment, as I looked at Oliver, I realized two things.

The first was that he did not hate me at all. In fact, he very much looked like he might love me.

And the second was that I was afraid that I might feel the same.

But I couldn't say any of that. It was too heavy. Too much.

I was too much. Such a declaration would ruin this dinner that was meant for spending time with friends.

So, instead, I said, "I'm thankful for all of you."

A beat of silence followed in which you could've heard a pin drop.

Had I said something wrong?

Jameson cleared his throat a moment later, before lifting his wine glass. "To love, family, and new beginnings."

Everyone *plinked* their glasses together before taking a drink. Then we all dug into the food.

"How's college, Emma?" Elsie asked through a mouthful of food. "You graduate soon, right?"

Emma's face lit up. "Yep! It's been great. I love it so much. The classes are fascinating, and once I graduate in the spring, I found a paid internship accompanying some storm chasers when tornado season starts."

The blood drained from Jameson's face. "I'm sorry, what?"

Emma rolled her eyes. "Don't worry, Jam-Jam. I'll be fine. We stay at a distance, so I won't *actually* be in any danger."

"Have you discussed this with mom?"

She snorted. "Of course not. She doesn't need that kind of stress."

"So, you admit it's something to stress about."

Emma set her fork down. "Jameson, I will be perfectly safe, I promise. But you know how mom would worry."

"Like how *I* will now be worrying."

Emma just laughed, waving him off.

Elsie tried to change the subject to get that stricken look off Jameson's face. "Have you met any boys on that fancy college campus of yours?"

Some of the joy leaked out of Emma's expression and she looked at her plate, poking at her potatoes.

"No, I'm focusing on my schoolwork."

Jameson and I locked eyes, recognizing it for the lie it was.

There was one boy Emma had always had her eye on—ever since she was little.

When Emma was younger, she had a childhood best friend, Liam. All of Meridel expected them to get married someday, at least until Liam signed a record deal and left with barely a goodbye last year.

Knowing we were drifting into territory she didn't like venturing into, I had mercy on her and changed the subject. "How long are you staying, Em?"

She gave me a grateful look. "I'll head back to the city in a few days. Since Jamie will be out of town and mom's strength is getting better, I'm going to bring her back to the city with me, show her around campus."

"We'll have to get coffee and catch up before you leave," I said before Elsie and Jameson hijacked the conversation, launching into talking about wedding plans.

Elsie had asked me to be her maid of honor, which I was ecstatic about, but I was certain I had heard all their plans at least ten times by now, so my mind started to wander as they filled in Emma on the venue and details.

Oliver's hand, which was still on my knee, started inching higher up my thigh, his thumb moving in tiny circles. I turned questioning eyes on him, silently asking him what he was doing, but his gaze burned through me, and I had to look away.

His hand continued to drift higher, and I slapped my hand down on his. He laced his pinky with mine. A strange silence fell over the table.

"Maya, can you help me get more wine?" Emma asked me, rising from her chair.

I quirked a brow. "Uh, sure."

Oliver's hand slid from my leg as I followed her into the kitchen.

"So, what's the story with you and Oliver?" Emma asked, spinning on me.

"What?"

"There's clearly something going on between you two. You look like you're undressing each other with your eyes, yet you have very different answers on who you are to each other, so give me the scoop."

My face grew hot at her assessment.

I sighed, wishing once again that I could've told her this weeks ago. "We're fake dating."

"*Fake* dating? Why would you do that?"

Withholding a groan, I caught Emma up on everything that had happened the last few weeks; that I offered to be Oliver's fake girlfriend, our date at the Christmas tree farm, and our first kiss in his Jeep during the snowstorm. When I finished, Emma's eyes were wide.

"I picked a crappy time to have college finals," she muttered which made me snort. "How are you handling this?"

Normally I loved that Emma could see through me, having watched me go through all the pain and heartache first with my dad and then my mom. She was the type of person who just *sensed* what others were feeling, or if something was off.

But right now, when I was already so conflicted over Oliver, I wished she wasn't so aware.

"I'm...handling it," I lied. Maybe there would be time for us to catch up and dissect all these feelings I'd been having, but not when Oliver was in the next room. Not when we were supposed to be spending Friendsmas together. "We should head back in," I suggested.

She stopped me with a hand on my arm. "Just tell me this. Why are you *fake* dating when you've been flinging flirty looks at each other all evening?"

The breath caught in my throat. "Err, what?"

"You're trying to fight it, but you forget that I know you well, Maya. I know when you like someone."

The blood drained from my face. "It's all pretend, Em." Maybe if I said it enough times, it would become true. "We're just putting on a show so we can be convincing at his family dinner."

Emma snorted again. "It's definitely been a show, but I think you should try harder." My cousin winked at me. *Winked.*

Dang it, Emma. Why are you doing this?

"I really think we should get back to dinner," I begged, grabbing the bottle on the counter, and heading back to the table without waiting for my cousin.

Elsie was asking Oliver about his hobbies as we settled back down in our seats. Jameson gave us a funny look, like we were two misbehaving children. Conversation stuttered to a halt as wine glasses were refilled.

Jameson cleared his throat. "So, Maya, Els told me that you entered that—"

"OKAY, WHO'S READY FOR DESSERT?" I shouted, jumping to my feet. Jameson looked at me like I had grown two more heads.

I shoved my chair back and ran into the kitchen in search of any sweets I could find. I didn't know what they had planned for dessert, but at this point I would take powdered pudding mix and serve it on a fancy platter to keep Jameson from finishing that thought. Realizing I had feelings for Oliver made him finding out about the contest even more terrifying. It wouldn't be hard for him to put the pieces together to figure out I was using him.

Then how would he feel about me?

Everyone at the table was quiet, and I heard the distinct scrape of a chair on the floor before Oliver appeared in the doorway. I stood by the counter, my arms wrapped around my stomach.

"Sorry," I said.

Oliver stepped close to me. "For what?"

I shook my head. There were too many answers to that.

Even though I hadn't explained, and there was no way he could know why I was upset, Oliver pulled me into his arms, wrapping them around my back. My head settled on his chest, and I breathed in the scent of his cologne.

Why did I instantly melt into him? Why did his touch relax me when it should've made me want to run far away?

"Well, would you look at that," Elsie said in a sly voice from the doorway, and I startled, prompting Oliver to tighten his hold on me.

I thought she was referring to the way he was holding me, but when I lifted my head to look at her, she was looking above our heads.

We both looked up at the same time Elsie announced, "Mistletoe!"

I expected to feel dread, like I had when we did that fake kiss at the Christmas tree farm, but I found myself *wanting* to kiss Oliver beneath the mistletoe this time.

Jameson and Emma appeared behind Elsie. "Come on, let's see a kiss."

"A real one," Emma added.

Oliver smiled at me, his blue eyes lighting up. "Let's give them a proper mistletoe kiss, princess. None of that faking from before," he whispered.

I had barely nodded when his lips met mine. This was nothing like that mistletoe bluff. This was heat and desire and passion all rolled into one. I wasn't even embarrassed that my cousins and best friend were witnessing it.

Elsie gave a wolf whistle which made the other two laugh.

Oliver was slow to break the kiss, his lips lingering as long as possible. When my eyes fluttered open and I met his gaze, there was nothing fake about the way he looked at me. Nor was there anything fake about how I was feeling.

"That's more like it," Elsie said before she marched past us, grabbed a pie out of the fridge, and then they all left us alone in the kitchen.

My pulse pounded in my ears, and I couldn't hear anything else.

"Maya, I want to tell you something..." Oliver whispered, resting his forehead against mine.

I licked my lips, debating kissing him again, but

his next words had ice spreading through me while fire poured into my veins.

"Maya, I'm crazy about you."

Oliver

The words were out of my mouth before I could stop them; before I could think through whether this was the time to tell her. All I knew in that moment was that I *needed* to tell her—I needed her to know how I felt.

I didn't want *fake* anymore. I wanted real and raw and this passion between us that we kept forcing into a little cage.

I wanted to unlock that cage, burn it, and never look back.

Her blue eyes were wide as she blinked at me. "What?"

"I know it seems impossible, and maybe a little too fast, but I've felt this way for a long time. The moment I first saw you in that photography class, I was drawn to your vivacious personality and that smile that instantly made my day better, and all I wanted was to get close to you, talk to you, maybe tease you a little, even if you hated me for it."

Her eyes softened, and it spurred me to keep going.

"Driving you around has only solidified what I thought I felt about you. Maya, you are breathtaking. The way you see the world, the joy you exude despite the struggles you've gone through, the way you care for everyone else…you're incredible. Every moment with you has been the best of my life. I know you haven't been my biggest fan…but maybe somewhere in all this faking, maybe you have developed feelings for me too."

I couldn't interpret the look on her face. Her brows were low over her eyes, but her lips were parted, almost in disbelief. It wasn't quite happiness *or* disgust, the latter of which I took to be a good sign, even if I was disappointed that she wasn't throwing herself into my arms.

I understood that her childhood had made it difficult for her to trust people, and I was sure my confession was shocking to her—especially since she believed that I hated her all this time.

Before she could respond, Emma called from the living room.

"Hey! There's pie! And it's almost time for presents! Are you coming?"

Maya closed her eyes, taking a deep breath. "Yeah, we'll be right there," she replied. Then she turned apologetic eyes on me. "Can we talk about this later, Oliver?"

I didn't want to talk about it later, I wanted to talk about it *now*, but this wasn't the right time. I swallowed before giving a small nod, not trusting my tongue to behave, and she held my stare for a few heartbeats. When she pulled away, I had to force my fingers to let go of her.

Back in the living room, Elsie handed us each a plate of chocolate cream pie and we all settled on the floor next to the Christmas tree. Jameson's dog was curled up in the corner, tail wagging and tongue lolling.

A few presents were nestled under the tree, and I fished out Maya's gift from my pocket and placed it with the others when she wasn't looking.

"Merry Christmas," Elsie said to her fiancé, handing him the first gift.

He unwrapped the box to reveal a pocket watch with a note engraved on the inside.

Jameson squinted to read, "Wear on our wedding day," before he laughed. "No 'I love you' or 'I can't wait to spend forever with you'?" he asked her.

"You already know those things. This seemed more practical. And now you won't forget."

Jameson laughed again and pulled Elsie in for a quick kiss.

Then he gave both her and Maya gift certificates to a spa for several services I had never heard of. "Now you two can pamper yourselves before the wedding."

Elsie gave him another kiss while Maya beamed and

said, "Thanks, Jam-Jam."

Emma gave her brother a giant Iowa State sweatshirt. "So you can think of me when I'm away." She flicked her hair over her shoulder and Jameson smiled at her.

"I always think of you, Em. Thank you."

Elsie stole the sweatshirt from his hands. "I'll be wearing that."

"I'd expect nothing less," he said through a laugh.

Then he handed Emma a little box. "It's from me and mom."

Emma gasped as she opened the present and pulled out a pair of tickets.

"I remember you mentioning that new severe weather convention thing happening next year with all those nerds and forums," Jameson explained. "There's two tickets so you can take someone with you."

Emma giggled at his description, but her eyes shimmered with gratitude. "Thanks, Jam-Jam."

I leaned over and asked Maya, "What's with the nickname?"

She chuckled, whispering back, "It was a funny name we called Jameson when he was a teen and loved to play guitar. It started as a joke but now it's his special term of endearment." Her lips brushed the shell of my ear as she talked, and goosebumps covered my arms.

Then she pulled away to grab another gift and handed it to Emma who ripped into it to reveal a shirt that said "I take weather cirrusly" which made her laugh. Then Maya gave Elsie a photo album of her favorite pictures from that stranger photoshoot that brought Elsie and Jameson together. Elsie and Emma both gave Maya a new strap for her camera.

"You can never have too many straps," Maya laughed before hugging them both.

I expected it to be awkward sitting there while everyone opened gifts, but it was strangely enjoyable. I loved watching how they all interacted, like a true family, and seeing their faces light up when they received a thoughtful gift.

My family Christmases were never like that. My mum tried, she really did, but with a man like my dad in the house, it was never like *this*. There weren't tender moments or sincere gratitude. It was always robotic, a going-through-the-motions tradition that he suffered through until he could go back to doing whatever it was he did when he was away from us.

Over the years, my mum and I created our own Christmas traditions, which I loved, but there was always a tinge of sadness—like something was missing. It wasn't the same as *this*.

I glanced at Maya again, her face lit up with laughter as Emma said something mildly offensive to her brother. The breath was stolen from my lungs at the sight of her smile. I wanted this—this loving feeling of family, of belonging—and I wanted it with Maya.

Then it was my turn to give Maya her gift. Why was my pulse thundering in my chest?

I handed the tiny box to her, and she gave me a look that I couldn't quite decipher.

"You didn't need to get me anything, Oliver."

"I wanted to," I answered with a small smile.

Everyone went quiet as Maya unwrapped the paper and held the little black box in her hand. At first glance, someone might think it was a ring box. Her gaze flicked to mine, questioning.

I kept that smile plastered to my face because I was afraid that my fear would show if I didn't.

Maya opened the box, and she went still like a marble statue, blinking several times before looking back at me, that strange look back on her face. For a moment, everything and everyone in the room faded away and it was just the two of us, eyes locked on each other.

"What is it?" Emma blurted, cracking through the moment.

Maya blinked then lifted the box's contents out and held it up.

"Aww," Elsic and Emma said at the same time.

It was a necklace with a small, rose gold polaroid camera on it. The necklace was dainty, but it had screamed *Maya*. I paid extra to have the shop engrave her name on the charm to make it even more special.

It wasn't anything fancy, but it *was* made just for her.

"Here, let's put it on," Elsie said, moving to help Maya with the clasp.

A moment later the necklace was shining on her

neck. Pleasure rushed through me seeing something I had given her against her skin.

"It's beautiful," Elsie commented, tossing a secretive look at Jameson.

Maya's eyes were shimmering as she looked at me and said, "Thank you, Oliver."

"You're welcome."

I wanted to kiss her. More than anything.

Our thoughts must have been aligned because then she crawled over to me and planted a kiss on my lips. Surprised chuckles filled the room as she pulled back. Her wide eyes made me think she was just as surprised by her actions as everyone else was.

Then a mischievous smile curled her lips. "Your turn." She reached behind the tree, where a small gift had been hiding.

"Maya…"

I hadn't been expecting anything at all, least of all from her.

Her answering smile was like my own personal sunshine.

"I wanted to," she repeated my words.

My own hands trembled as I slipped the ribbon off and ripped open the present. I sucked in a breath. It was a small wooden picture frame, and inside it was a photo of…me. It was a partial side-shot, taken from a distance. My camera was up at my face, but beneath it I was smiling. The way the photo captured the light and landscape around me told me everything I needed to know about the photographer.

Maya had taken this photo of me, and based on the fresh, white snow around me and the clothes I was wearing, she must have taken it this morning during the engagement shoot.

I couldn't remember Maya turning her camera on me at all, but perhaps she'd been sneaky about it.

It wasn't the fact that she had taken a photo of me and framed it that rocked me to my core, but instead it was the *way* she captured me. For the first time in months, maybe even years, I looked like I was enjoying photography again, rather than doing it for a paycheck. Even with half my face hidden behind a camera, Maya had managed to paint me in a new light.

It was beautiful.

Was this how she saw *me*?

I swallowed against the lump in my throat as I met Maya's gaze.

"Thank you, darling." Those words were not enough, and yet it was all I could manage. I leaned forward and pressed a kiss to her lips, hoping that conveyed everything I didn't know how to say.

Her eyes were slow to flutter open as I pulled away. Jameson, Elsie, and Emma sat watching us with wide, enraptured eyes.

I cleared my throat. "Happy Christmas, everyone." Since I didn't have a drink to raise, I grabbed the closest thing—a forkful of pie—and lifted it into the air. There were a few chuckles but a moment later everyone lifted their own pie-filled forks and murmured, "Merry Christmas."

I didn't know what the Christmas dinner with my family would bring, but I did know one thing. Spending the holiday with Maya and her people—there was no where I'd rather be. Whatever the future held, I would face it knowing that, if just for a moment, I had held Maya, kissed her, and celebrated a special day with her and the others. They barely knew me, but they had been so welcoming that I felt like I belonged here—with them.

That was something no one could take away.

Not even my father.

Maya

"**S**o, why haven't you told Oliver you entered that photo contest?" Elsie asked me after I had filled her in on everything that had happened recently. We were washing the dishes and Jameson and Emma were in the living room with Oliver participating in a great American past time: Scrabble.

I bit my lip, toweling off the last of the plates. "I'm scared."

Elsie's brows rose. "Maya—the great love guru—is scared?"

I smacked at her arm. "I don't want him to think I'm using him."

"But you *are* using him."

"Shh," I shushed, putting a finger to her lips. "Not so

loud." I peeked out the doorway. Oliver was still sitting on the floor, watching as Jameson and Emma smack-talked each other even though Oliver was clearly winning. As if he sensed me looking, he glanced over his shoulder and gave me a lopsided smile.

It made my heart do a strange little flop.

"Maya?" Elsie asked, breaking my focus on him.

I sighed. "It started off that way, yeah. But…" I pulled her farther into the kitchen so we wouldn't be overheard. "Els, he told me he's *crazy about me*," I whispered.

I managed to cover her mouth before her gasp alerted all three people in the next room. She let out a squeal of delight beneath my palm, and I shushed her again.

"I'm going to repeat what you said to me all those months ago," she said when I removed my hand. "Ahem." She made a show of clearing her throat before she said in a whiny voice, that I assumed was supposed to sound like me, "Oliver told you he has feelings for you. Why are you freaking out?"

I rolled my eyes. "And I'll repeat what you said to me—there weren't supposed to be feelings involved."

Elsie scoffed. "A little late for that."

"He's my archnemesis, Els. This wasn't supposed to happen. I was perfectly content to hate Oliver Lewis."

"*Was*? As in…you *no longer* hate him?"

I ran a hand through my curls. "I don't know what I feel."

Elsie made a *tsk* sound. "I think you do. You just

don't want to admit it. And I think that's why you don't want him to know about the contest. You think he'll walk away if he finds out you're using him."

"I'm not using him," I was quick to say, even though it was a lie. "Or at least...I don't want to be. He told me his dad has used his talent to get ahead for years. I don't want to be like that. I don't want to hurt him."

A slow smile spread across her face. "Maya, it sounds like you share Oliver's feelings."

My tongue was heavy in my mouth, and I couldn't muster an answer.

"You're not the type to let anything, or anyone, get in your way, or feel bad about it. The fact that you do tells me you don't want to lose him, which further tells me you have feelings for him."

The thought of losing Oliver had tears burning at the back of my eyes.

Crap. Was she right?

Elsie pulled me into a hug, squeezing me tight, helping to hold me together while I tried to understand what the heck I was feeling.

"You should tell him how you feel *and* about the contest," she said, and I sniffled into her shoulder. "It's better to tell him now than to keep it hidden and hope he doesn't find out later. Besides, wouldn't you rather be *happy*, Maya, instead of fighting against your feelings just because you *think* you're supposed to hate him? What if he makes you happy?"

"But what if *he* wins the contest and I'm left alone and broke again? Or what if I win and he finds out that I used him, and he hates me instead?"

Elsie shook her head as she leaned back to look at me. "Based on what I've seen tonight, I think he would sooner drop out of the contest altogether than risk losing you. Give him a chance. Don't expect the worst from him." She glanced over my shoulder at the man in question. "He just might surprise you."

The sound of Emma and Jameson's trash talking grew louder before they burst into the kitchen. Jameson went right for Elsie, hugging her from behind. Oliver was slow to follow, leaning against the doorway. There was something strange in his gaze as our eyes locked—something that made it impossible to look away.

Oliver Lewis told me he had feelings for me.

This should have rocked me to my core, shaking the foundations that I had built our mutual hatred on. But, instead, it was a strange, peaceful acceptance that eased the jagged edges inside me.

I didn't know if I was *in love* with Oliver, but I had a feeling I was well on my way.

As my cousins and best friend bantered back and forth over who was a better snowman builder, I crossed the kitchen and walked straight up to Oliver.

Everything I wanted to say stalled on my tongue. I'd never felt at such a loss for words before. His blue eyes burned straight through me, lighting me up from the inside out.

Not knowing what else to do, I stepped into his embrace, my hands gripping his shirt and pulled him down for a smoldering kiss. The others went silent behind me, but I hardly noticed. Not when Oliver's hands lit little fires on my back as he pulled me closer.

It was either two seconds or an eternity later when Emma cleared her throat, forcing Oliver to pull away.

"As great as it is watching you two make out in my brother's kitchen, there's still one last thing we have to do tonight," Emma said.

My cheeks warmed as I turned to face the others. Jameson's mouth was twisted in an amused expression, while Elsie had a smug look on her face that said *I told you so*.

Emma, on the other hand, looked annoyed. Her arms were crossed over her chest, her foot tapping the floor as she gave me a sassy raise of her eyebrows.

"Is it time?" Elsie asked.

"Oh, it's time," Emma replied in a dramatic voice.

"Time for what?" I asked, confused. We had already done dinner and dessert and presents. What more could there be?

A mischievous grin spread across my cousin's face. "It's time…"

Jameson chuckled.

"For?" I prodded.

"For…" The smile was still on Emma's face.

I sighed, tilting my head back to look at the ceiling. I loved my cousin to death, but she had a habit of being melodramatic.

"IT'S TIME TO BUILD A SNOWMAN!" Emma cried, throwing her hands into the air as if she expected a round of applause.

Elsie and Jameson snorted.

"Really, Em?" I asked, unable to keep the cynicism out of my voice.

"What's wrong with building a snowman? It's a Beck family tradition."

Jameson cocked his head. "We've never built a snowman at Christmas before."

"It's a *new* tradition."

It was my turn to snort. "How convenient."

Emma rolled her eyes. "Come on. There's fresh snow outside and I don't get to see you guys that often. Let's see who can build the best—"

"—or ugliest—" Jameson whispered to Elsie.

"—snowman!"

When no one said anything, Emma stalked over to me and looped our arms together.

"Come on, Maya. We can beat these yahoos."

"Yahoos?" Oliver asked. The goofy word was far too adorable in his accent.

I giggled. "It basically means an ignorant rural person. It's a Midwestern thing." I patted him on the shoulder as I passed him, and I didn't miss the smoldering look he gave me in return.

The five of us pulled on a ridiculous amount of snow gear before wobbling like penguins outside in the dark, Luna trailing after us with her tail wagging. The moon reflected off the snow making the landscape sparkle, while the cold air froze the snot in our nostrils.

"Okay," Emma said, clapping her gloved hands together with a dull *thud*. "Couples against couples, and I'll be the judge!"

Elsie pursed her lips. "How is that fair?"

"Well, it would be an unfair advantage to whichever team had *me* helping, so I'll just even the playing field and take myself out of the game."

Jameson rubbed at his temple.

Emma was something else.

"Elsie and Jam-Jam, you go over there," she pointed to the left, "and Maya and Oliver, you stay right here. First couple to build a complete snowman wins. And try to make them unique."

Before I could even think about what would qualify as a unique snowman, Emma shouted, "Go!"

The four of us stood there, staring at Emma like she had lost her mind.

"What are you waiting for? These snowmen won't build themselves!" Then Emma bent and gathered up a snowball and chucked it at Jameson, hitting him square in the chest. He looked down at the snow covering his coat before quirking a brow at his sister. Elsie stifled a giggle behind a gloved hand.

"Forget the snowmen!" Elsie cried before stooping to gather her own snowball. "Snowball fight!" Then she threw it at me. I barely managed to duck as it zoomed overhead before smacking Oliver's shoulder.

I looked up from where I was crouched in front of him, his eyes flashing as they met mine. For a second, I thought he was angry. But then, with slow, deliberate movements, he took off his glasses, speckled with snow from the impact, and put them safely in an inner pocket in his coat before he bent down and gathered snow into his hands.

And then he dunked it on top of my head.

Everything sped up as all five of us dove into the snow, building as many snowballs as we could before unleashing them on each other. Luna romped around us, riled up from our frantic movements and little screams. Snow was everywhere—in my coat, in my gloves and boots, but I didn't care. All I saw were Oliver's blue eyes glowing in the moonlight, and the smile on his face as he joined my family in a snowball fight.

It was everything I never knew I wanted.

And in that moment I realized I couldn't let Oliver get away because I was crazy about him too.

22

Oliver

I didn't know it was possible to have every inch of my body frozen while my insides blazed.

Even though I had been wearing winter gear, every inch of fabric was soaked through. The snowball fight had lasted for a full hour. I was sore in places I didn't know could *get* sore, and by the way everyone shuffled around the room, I wasn't alone.

When we were all reduced to giant shaking masses, the five of us retreated inside and huddled around the fireplace where Jameson had stoked a fire. All the wet snow gear sat in a pile by the door. Jameson's dog looked at us like we were all a bunch of wimps even though she was soaking wet too.

Maya's blonde hair dripped cold droplets onto the

floor, her entire body shaking from head to toe. Elsie disappeared into Jameson's room for a moment before appearing with an armful of clothes.

"Here." She dropped them in front of us. "They'll probably be huge on everyone but Oliver, but at least they'll be dry and warm."

Emma wasted no time snatching a T-shirt and sweatpants and ran down the short hall to the bathroom. Elsie and Jameson took turns changing next, and then it was just Maya and me.

I took her hand and pulled her to her feet. "Come on, let's get you in some dry clothes." I expected her to argue or say something sassy, as per usual, but she stumbled after me as I carried the clothes for her.

She walked into the bathroom first, setting the clothes on the counter and I made to close the door to give her privacy when she laid a hand on mine. The cold-induced foggy look disappeared from her eyes as she looked at me. She guided me closer until our chests were almost touching.

My wet clothes were frigid against my skin, but it was lost in the back of my mind as Maya skimmed her fingers up my arm and then brushed them against the stubble on my face.

"Maya…"

We were both shivering and sopping wet from the snow, in a tiny, cramped bathroom, but all I wanted was to lift her onto the counter and kiss her senseless. Somehow sensing my thoughts, Maya leaned onto her toes and pressed her soft lips to mine. Her nose bumped my glasses. She smiled against my lips and gently removed them, setting them on the counter.

If the Maya I had kissed all the previous times had been undecided about me, this had to have been "all in" Maya. There was no hesitation in the way she held onto me and pulled me toward her, desperate to be closer. There was no question in her body language as she put everything into that kiss. Did that mean she shared my feelings? I had a hard time believing she would kiss me like that if she didn't.

Why are you overthinking this, you fool? Just enjoy it.

I put my hands on her waist and lifted her onto the bathroom counter. Her legs wrapped around mine, her lips never breaking contact.

Maya tasted like chocolate pie and snow, an odd combination, but the more I tasted, the more I wanted. Her fingers played with the bottom of my shirt, skimming the skin above my pants, erasing every ounce of cold from my body.

This is what I wanted. A lifetime of heated kisses, and a feisty woman that kept me on my toes.

Maya Beck was it for me.

"Ahem."

We broke apart faster than lightning.

Emma stood in the doorway with her arms crossed, her head cocked as she looked between the two of us.

"I was just coming to make sure y'all had the clothes you needed, but it looks like you haven't even gotten that far."

Maya's cheeks were bright red as she hopped down off the counter. "We're good."

I grabbed my glasses, nearly poking myself in the eye as I struggled to put them back on, then my clothes, and stepped out of the bathroom. Maya closed the door a moment later. As I walked down the hall to change in one of the bedrooms, Emma stepped in front of me.

For the first time all evening, she glared at me. "Don't hurt her."

Nerves prickled like needles under my skin. "Pardon?"

Emma didn't back down, her hands fisting at her sides. "Maya has been through enough people abandoning her in her life. She doesn't need anyone else to break her heart."

"Emma, I would never hurt her. I'm..." I sighed. "I'm in love with Maya." The truth of the words snapped through me. Nothing had ever felt so right.

"Love makes people do strange things. People leave all the time *in the name of love*."

I rubbed the back of my neck. "I don't intend on leaving, Emma. Not unless she wants me to."

She arched a brow.

I took it a step further. "I left my life in England behind just for a chance of seeing her again. I can't get her out of my head, nor do I want to. If she'll have me, I don't plan on walking away from her ever again."

Emma's eyes widened, silence descending in the hallway before she sighed.

"Maya has a big heart, Oliver. She spends so much time helping others that it often comes at the cost of taking care of herself. She puts her heart on the line only to have it cracked and shattered. Don't be one of those people."

I lifted my chin, taking her words as a challenge. "I would never."

"I hope you're telling the truth, or so help me you'll never find Meridel to be a welcoming place again."

Her words sent an eerie chill through my body that had nothing to do with the fact that I was still in wet clothes. Though Emma was tall, she wasn't the type of person I would have been afraid of, but something about her words, and the protective, no-nonsense way she threatened me had me backing up a step.

Emma is a little frightening.

The bathroom door opened, and Maya emerged, freezing when she saw us standing there. Her eyes narrowed as she looked between the two of us, our bodies tense from the conversation.

"What's going on?" she asked, crossing her arms over the giant T-shirt that went to her knees.

"Nothing," Emma sang before bouncing back into the living room.

Not wanting to admit to Maya that her cousin was

a little scary, I just gave her a smile and slipped behind her into the bathroom to change. When I came back out, Maya, Emma, and Elsie were piled on the couch, each nursing a mug of hot chocolate, while Jameson sat in a modern version of a bean bag chair on the floor.

As scary as it was risking my heart on someone who had been adamant about hating me for the past year, I felt a sense of belonging here, even despite Emma's warning. I had spent a single evening with these people, and I already adored them. I hated the thought of saying goodbye or never seeing them again.

I wanted Maya and this goofy family of hers.

What I told Emma was the truth. I wasn't going anywhere. Not unless Maya asked me to.

The rest of the evening passed in a blur as the four of them fell into an easy rhythm, trading jests and poking fun at each other.

I had never experienced anything like this.

I was an only child, and it was just me, my dad, and mum for much of my life. I never had close cousins, and once I got older and started traveling more often, it didn't leave room for having many friends.

Christmas was always a tense holiday in the Lewis household. It was just another chance for my father to be rude and belittle me and the choices I'd made for my life.

The words I had said to Maya at the Christmas tree farm about this being a time to celebrate the people that *are* with us, while true, was something that I, too, struggled with. I was trying to make her feel better, but I related to her. My parents might not have abandoned me, but I'd never felt like I belonged, even in my own family.

But here, with Maya and her family, even though I wasn't technically a part of theirs, I still felt a sense of belonging, of acceptance.

My heart ached over all the heartbreak Maya had gone through. Yes, my relationship with my father was strained, but at least neither of my parents had walked out on me. Though I hated going to them or relying on them for anything, at least I knew they were there if I needed them. I couldn't imagine growing up without that support.

It only proved how strong this woman was, that she faced so much, overcame all that should have destroyed her, and still held onto that spark of life.

Maya laughed at something Jameson said, her blonde hair spilling over her shoulder as she threw her head back in sheer joy.

I never wanted that expression to fall off her face.

I would do whatever it took to keep it there.

Another hour passed, the moon high overhead when we left, and I drove Maya back to her apartment. Within moments of getting in the car, her eyes slipped closed, and she fell asleep. Each time the Jeep rolled to a stop I couldn't help glancing over at her. A life with her flashed behind my eyes, I saw it all perfectly.

Chasing our dreams, growing a business, building a

home, and starting a family, experiencing all that life had to offer *together*.

I wanted it so bad my heart ached.

Careful not to wake her, I took her hand from her lap and kissed the back of it, wishing I never had to let go.

Maya might not return my feelings yet, but I knew without a doubt...

This woman was my forever.

23

Maya

On Christmas Eve I woke up with that familiar sense of dread that made my stomach roil and squeezed the air from my lungs, making it difficult to breathe.

I had always hated this day. It was a day where we, as a family, should have been wrapping up presents, baking some cookies, or having a Christmas movie marathon. But instead, it was a day that I wondered where my father had gone, and questioned whether my mom would even come home, or if she'd keep wasting her life working and ignoring me.

I had learned to hate Christmas Eve because it meant I was always alone. As sad and pathetic as it sounded, it was a day where it was evident that I had no one that loved me enough to be their first choice.

Even when Aunt Maggie started inviting me to spend Christmas with them a few years ago, I was still alone on Christmas Eve. I would wake up on Christmas morning and see a sad little tree that I had put up by myself, with zero presents under it—at least until I stopped bothering to decorate at all.

I didn't waste money buying my mom gifts anymore. I learned the hard way that she neither wanted them nor cared whether she received anything from me or not.

Still sore from the snowball fight, I half rolled half fell out of my bed with a weird combination of a whimper and a groan before shuffling into the kitchen. Usually, I was happy to see my place void of any reminders of what time of year it was, but this year it made my heart throb.

A dull ache filled my chest. My limbs were far too heavy as I made a pot of coffee then collapsed on the couch with my mug.

It had been a weird couple of days since Friendsmas. Elsie, Jameson, and Luna took off on their trip, and Emma left with Aunt Maggie to drive back to the city.

I had offered to keep Emma company while she was still in Meridel, but she claimed she had a lot of homework to do. "Weather never sleeps," she'd said. Though I suspected that was a fib. Emma was wallowing. She likely wanted to be alone because being back in Meridel after Liam had left brought back bad memories.

So, I spent the last two days at home since Dina's was

closed this week. I still didn't have a car, so I couldn't go anywhere, and after Oliver's confession and the tender way he kissed me when he dropped me off at home, I couldn't bring myself to talk to him. Though that didn't stop him from texting me multiple times asking if I was all right, or if I wanted to *practice* for his family dinner some more.

Eventually I responded and asked for some alone time, feeling like a terrible person for doing so. I didn't need alone time. I was just too scared to face my feelings—and Oliver. I had no regrets about what happened at Friendsmas, but I couldn't face my feelings. It was easier to shove them away and pretend they didn't exist than face them and the possibility of a shattered heart.

The irony was, after everything I had experienced with Oliver over the last couple of weeks, I didn't think he would break my heart.

And somehow that made it even scarier.

And it was weird—the way I found myself missing him. It was a feeling I wasn't used to; different from how I missed anyone else in my life. This was overwhelming, like I was missing a crucial piece of me, and something *more* that I didn't know how to identify.

I fought myself on several occasions, going back and forth on whether to see Oliver, but I never got myself to put fingers to the screen and send the message. His confession had shocked me, and my own feelings had as well, and I was still all over the place, trying to come to terms with what I felt for Oliver Lewis.

I had hated him for so long, so it was more than a little strange to *not* hate him and feel...*this*.

With nothing else to do, I flipped on the Hallmark Channel and lost myself in someone else's fantastical and romantic life when mine was confusing and indescribable. I had just started to doze off again, despite the two mugs of coffee I had, when my phone buzzed next to me.

BLASTED BRIT

Happy Christmas Eve, princess.

My stomach erupted into butterflies, but I couldn't help sending a snarky response, bitter about being alone *again* on Christmas Eve.

ME

I don't see anything particularly happy about today.

His response was quick.

BLASTED BRIT

Well, maybe we should change that.

ME

[GIF of a skeptical face]

BLASTED BRIT

You dare to question my skills to make you happy?

My fingers froze, hovering over the screen as I thought back on all the moments we had been together—when I had felt a new sort of happiness I'd never experienced before. As much as I hated to admit it, no, Oliver had no problem making me happy.

And therein lay the problem.

ME

Sigh how do you plan to make me happy, Oliver?

BLASTED BRIT

Mwhahahaha

ME

Did you just evil laugh?

BLASTED BRIT

And if I did?

ME

I am really starting to question your sanity.

BLASTED BRIT

I promise you, Maya, I am perfectly sane :)

I shall pick you up after lunch :)

ME

Shall? This isn't England, you know.

BLASTED BRIT

Oh, I know. England doesn't have you. And it's a real shame.

I swallowed hard, trying to squash the colony of butterflies returning to my stomach, thankful that he wasn't here to see my cheeks flaming.

ME

What are you planning, you blasted Brit?

BLASTED BRIT

I'm going to show you MY favorite way to spend Christmas Eve.

See you soon.

As promised, Oliver picked me up after lunch, opening the door to his Jeep for me with a big, goofy smile.

"Hi," I offered as I crawled in.

"Hello, princess." Somehow his smile widened even more, and the sight of it sent my heart into overdrive. I squeezed my knuckles, and Oliver took my hand, interlacing our fingers and giving them a soft peck.

"I'm glad you came," he said as if he'd given me a choice in the matter.

"I'm just here for the 'happy' you promised," I reminded him.

His grin turned mischievous. "Just you wait."

Twenty minutes later, we pulled into the driveway of Oliver's townhouse, and my stomach swooped.

"What are we doing here?" I asked, swallowing down my nerves.

Even though I had been to his house before, now that he had confessed how he felt about me, it carried more weight.

"I told you. I'm showing you how I like to spend today. Since our dinner isn't until tomorrow, and neither of us has anything else to do," he stopped to quirk a brow at me, daring me to argue, "then we might as well spend it together."

He wasn't *wrong*, so I didn't even bother denying it.

I was so relieved not to have to spend the day by myself that I didn't mind being here with him. There might have been more reasons too, but I wasn't about to examine them—not even with a thirty-nine-and-a-half-foot pole.

"What are we doing then?" I repeated my earlier question.

"If I told you, what would be the fun in that?"

"It would be loads of fun," I deadpanned.

Oliver's low chuckle had goosebumps erupting on my skin.

"Come on, Feisty Maya. I promise you'll enjoy today."

Oliver unlocked the door, took my hand, and dragged me inside where I came to a stop.

His home looked like Christmas had thrown up all over it.

Bright silver and red tinsel hung on the tree we had picked out a couple weeks ago and on every possible surface. It dangled from the mantle, down the stair banister, and in each of the doorways.

The sad little tree was lit up in blinking multicolored lights, though there weren't any ornaments on it, and two small presents were nestled beneath the boughs, one labeled *Mum* and the other *Dad*.

Various Christmas-themed trinkets were placed here and there, like a little red truck with tiny gifts in the bed sitting on the coffee table and a miniature Christmas village along the mantle.

"Wow," I said, at a loss for words.

"Too much?" he asked, his blue eyes shimmering in the twinkling lights.

Normally I would have said yes. Anything remotely resembling Christmas was too much for me. But here, with Oliver, it didn't feel that way.

It was just right.

I shook my head, giving him a smile. "It's perfect."

The joy that spread across his face was like watching a child open a box with a puppy in it. And *I* had put it there.

I found myself wanting to find another way to bring

such a smile to his face.

What is happening to me?

"Wait here," Oliver said before disappearing up the stairs. When he reappeared holding something behind his back, he said, "close your eyes."

I gave him a skeptical look but did as he said. A moment later, his body heat smothered me as he stepped close, putting something in my hands.

"Part one of Maya and Oliver's Christmas Eve," he explained, and I opened my eyes to find a small bundle wrapped in pink tissue paper with a little twine bow holding it together.

"What a nice bow."

Oliver chuckled. "Just open it, feisty pants."

My lips curled into a smile as I ripped the tissue paper open. It fell to the floor as I stared at a pair of striped flannel pajamas.

I cocked my head. *Why would he give me pajamas? How did he even know my size?*

Oliver laughed at the expression on my face. "Don't worry. Elsie picked them out for you."

"Come again?"

"I asked her at Friendsmas what kind of pajamas you'd like. I have a matching pair too," he explained, throwing a thumb over his shoulder at his bedroom.

"How'd you know I'd come to your house tonight?"

He shrugged. "I didn't, but I hoped you would."

I smiled. Who was this sweet, tenderhearted,

thoughtful man, and where did the sassy, snarky, and rude guy I hated disappear to?

"You have a matching pair?" I couldn't keep the amusement from my voice.

His smile was shy—the first time I'd ever seen such a look from him. He pushed up his glasses.

"It's a tradition I used to do with my mum as a child. We'd pick out matching pajamas and wear them all day long on Christmas Eve. It's been at least a decade since I've done this, but it always felt like Christmas magic to me, and I thought maybe we could recreate it with some magic of our own."

I almost bit out that Christmas magic didn't exist again, but the sincerity, the genuineness in his eyes stopped me. This tradition meant a lot to him.

And he wanted to share it with me.

Swoon!

"I'll go change," I said, heading toward the bathroom.

A few minutes later I emerged wearing the pajamas and found Oliver lounging on the couch in his own pair.

How was it possible for a pair of pajamas to fit someone so well? If he were a marble statue, he would have been named *Adonis in Flannel.*

I giggled to myself at the image in my head and Oliver smiled at me.

"What's so funny?"

I shook my head. "You're too handsome for your own good." I gasped as soon as the words slipped out—

my filter once again failing—and put a hand over my mouth.

Oliver pushed to his feet and approached me with an amused glint in his eyes. "You think I'm handsome?"

My heart and brain had two different responses as I shook my head at the same time I blurted, "Yes."

His fingers wrapped around my wrist, lowering it before he brushed my hair behind an ear.

"And I've never seen someone look as beautiful in flannel pajamas as you," he said, his voice low and gravelly. His touch combined with those words made my heart stutter, and he smiled like he knew the effect he was having on me.

Oliver leaned forward, giving my lips the barest caress with his.

It was everything.

And it was not enough.

He grinned as he pulled away, leaving me breathless.

"What's next?" I managed to squeak.

He bent down and lifted a box which emitted a loud rattling noise when he jostled it. "First, we're going to finish decorating the tree."

My heart swelled at the same time my stomach plummeted to the floor. Decorating Christmas trees was something I had grown to hate because I was always forced to do it alone since neither of my parents were ever around. It was one of the reasons why I didn't get my own tree.

I had told Oliver that. I had told him it wasn't fun to decorate alone.

He could have finished decorating the tree himself, but he had waited for this moment—with me.

This man kept rewriting my most painful memories and turning them into something beautiful again. I swallowed down the lump in my throat as he opened the noisy box and winced. Curious, I peeked inside. The ornaments were a tangled mess, all the metal hooks bent together to create a shining, glittery mass.

Oliver pushed his glasses up his nose, his ears turning red. "They didn't look like that when I put them in there."

I bit my lip to hold back a laugh and started working on untangling them. When we finished, we lovingly—and by that, I mean haphazardly—placed the ornaments on the tree, teasing and taunting each other over what went where, then stepped back to admire our handiwork.

"It's rather ugly," Oliver said.

I burst out laughing. "*Now* you see it. I'm proud of you, Oliver. Admitting is the first step to getting help," I teased, and he pinched my arm.

Through my giggles, I asked, "What's next?"

Oliver shoved the empty box into the hall closet before responding. "We could bake cookies or watch some Christmas movies," he offered, "or play a game. We always did something different every year."

I quirked a brow. "What kind of game?"

He pointed at his assortment of video game consoles

in the cabinet beneath his TV.

I gasped. "Oliver Lewis. Are you a secret gamer nerd?"

He pushed up his glasses again. "Not a secret nerd. A proud one."

Ugh. Oliver was hot enough as it was. How is it possible for him to get even hotter?

I nodded at the stack of games. "Pick one."

His brows rose. "You want to play video games with me?"

"More than anything." I paused, relishing the way he looked at me now, like I had just given him the world's best gift. "Just know I'll probably be terrible."

Oliver's smile was sweet. "Don't worry, princess. I'll go easy on you."

Maya

"**I** cannot believe you hustled me," Oliver said, exasperated after losing his tenth game of *Mario Kart* in a row. I folded a crisp twenty-dollar bill into the pocket of my pajamas with a sly smile. *That'll teach you to underestimate me.*

"I did say I'd *probably* be terrible."

His scowl made me giggle.

"You destroyed me."

"It's okay, Oliver. We can't all be good at everything."

His scowl deepened and I cackled.

"I need some chocolate," he muttered before throwing the controller on the couch and heading into the kitchen.

"Have the roles reversed, dear Oliver?" I called after him. "I beat you at video games and now *you* need chocolate to make yourself feel better?"

Oliver's unamused face peeked out from behind the cupboard door. "Don't make me come over there."

The way he growled it made it the sexiest threat I'd ever received, even if he was holding a container full of chocolate chips in his hands.

"Or what?" I taunted.

Very, very slowly, Oliver closed the cabinet, set the chocolate down on the counter before stalking across the living room, stopping right in front of me.

I wasn't sure if the look on his face meant he was about to pounce or burst into laughter. Then he did the last thing I expected.

He jumped onto the couch, straddling my lap, and started tickling the heck out of me. I tried not to laugh, I really did, but he found all the spots that were the most ticklish. He was relentless, a devious smile on his face the entire time until we both dissolved into fits of laughter.

We just had a tickle fight.

This sassy man was an absolute teddy bear. I never thought I'd like the cinnamon roll type of guy, but Oliver Lewis had me sold.

After he stopped, we were wrapped up in each other's arms. He pecked a light kiss to my cheek.

"If this is the reward, you can beat me at Mario Kart any day," he murmured against my skin. His lips brushed mine before he pulled himself off the couch, and I pressed mine together to keep from begging him to stay.

The daylight had disappeared, and Oliver peeked outside, rubbing his hands together. "It's time for my favorite part." He headed over to the fireplace where he put a few logs in and started a fire.

"A fire is your favorite part of Christmas Eve?" I asked.

He nodded as he went to the basket next to the couch, grabbed an unnecessary number of blankets and tossed them on the floor in front of the hearth. He made quick work of laying them out before he threw a few pillows down too.

"What are you doing?"

Oliver's smile was full of so much joy that I smiled back.

"The best part of our Christmas Eve tradition was always making a bed of blankets in front of the fire, munching on popcorn and cookies, then talking for hours until Christmas finally came. Then we'd fall asleep as the embers cooled and sleep until it was time to open presents."

The distinct sting of loss, like being stung by a wasp, pierced through me. He would lay on the floor for hours, just talking to his mom? How many times had I wished for such a thing? To be able to spend time with my own mom, to talk with her, ask her questions about life?

My eyes burned, and I forced myself to look away from him. But, of course, Oliver missed nothing and was there in an instant, his hands cradling my face.

"What is it, darling?"

I gave him a wobbly smile unable to keep the words I had locked up inside anymore. "It doesn't take much sometimes to realize all I missed out on." Oliver's eyes softened. "Sometimes it hits at weird times, and I have to start grieving all over again." I blinked. Had I ever said anything like that to anyone before?

"I'm so sorry, Maya. I wish I could erase that pain for you. But, perhaps, this is a chance to make *our* own traditions, our own memories—bright, happy ones that wipe away all the ones that cause us hurt."

He wiped a tear away with his thumb. "I learned a long time ago that my father will never be the man he should be, that he'll never be the type of father I needed or wanted him to be. Once I accepted that, I became happier. Otherwise, I lived in perpetual disappointment and anger."

"But how do you do that?"

"By taking it one day at a time, princess."

He made it sound so simple even though it wasn't. But I supposed he was right. One day at a time. It wasn't something that could be fixed in a single moment or wished away. It was a day by day, little by little type of healing, until it was no longer a suffocating feeling anymore; until there was a sense of acceptance that was endurable.

Oliver's words were a lifeline and a gift—one I didn't know I needed until that moment.

He pulled me up from the couch and wrapped me

in a hug.

"Why do you call me princess?" I asked after a moment. I had always thought it was just his way of being sassy, but maybe it had turned into something more meaningful.

His lips twitched at the corners, but he ducked his head, suddenly bashful. "Because you're important to me, Maya."

Such a simple reason. Yet, it had my knees weakening beneath me. If it weren't for the hold he had on my face, I might have collapsed to the floor.

"I'm really glad you're here," he whispered. He pressed a soft kiss to my forehead before diving onto the blankets and pillows, patting the ground for me to join him. I sank to my knees, laying across from him so our faces were close together.

I imagined we were quite the sight. Both wearing matching pajamas, wrapped in blankets, and lying on our stomachs next to a fire, a Christmas tree sparkling next to us.

For a long moment, we didn't speak, content to watch the fire and enjoy each other's company. The need to tell him about the contest was too much to contain. I wanted him to know. I didn't want to use him. I didn't want to hurt him. And I didn't want him to leave.

Maybe if I was honest with him about how much I needed the prize money, he'd understand.

I opened my mouth to tell him, but no sound would

come out. The words fled, and I couldn't speak around the lump in my throat.

"Can I tell you a something?" I managed to whisper, staring at the flames dancing around each other.

"Anything," Oliver replied.

I hesitated, still unable to get the confession to slide off my tongue. Why couldn't I just tell him I entered *Rising Star?*

In the end, I couldn't bring myself to do it. I was a coward, and settled for telling him a different secret instead.

"When I was a kid, I would stare up at the stars when I was alone on Christmas Eve, and just...watch. Wish. I wished for someone to love me enough to stay. I wished for someone to see me and want me for no other reason than because I'm me." I paused as my breath caught in my throat, and Oliver laced his fingers with mine, raising them up between us to kiss them.

"Every year that wish went unanswered, swallowed up by the endless black night. Every year...until this year." I turned my gaze from the flames to look at him. "I don't know what you've done to me, Oliver, but I'm helpless to stop it. I thought I hated you...and I've fought so hard to *keep* hating you. But I just...don't."

Oliver smiled but didn't say anything, letting me think through my next words.

I let out a long breath. "I don't know if I'm where you are yet, Oliver..."

"That's okay—"

"But I think I'm getting there."

His wide eyes blinked several times behind his glasses before the brightest smile lit up his face, giving the Christmas tree behind him a run for its money.

And then he kissed me.

"That's all—" he pecked a kiss to my nose, "I ever—" a kiss to my forehead, "wanted," a kiss to my neck. He pulled back to look at me. "A chance, Maya. I only wanted a chance."

It was my turn to smile. "I think I can give you that."

The words were surprising, even to me. Outside of Elsie and my cousins, I never let anyone get close enough, never gave anyone else a chance. Because letting people get close meant the possibility of them leaving.

But something about Oliver, the way he was with me and how he treated me, had me thinking that maybe he was different. That maybe he wouldn't leave like everyone before him.

It made me *want* to give him a chance.

I wasn't ready to tell him that I loved him. I'd save those three words for a day when I couldn't hold them back any longer.

But I was ready to make us something *more*, something real.

As if sensing my inner decision, Oliver kissed me, and I lost track of time as we laid there on the floor of his townhouse next to a roaring fire and a twinkling Christmas tree, lost in each other's arms, and the beauty we had managed to find.

Maya

The sunrise peeked through the curtains in a gentle caress as Christmas morning fell upon us. I wasn't a morning person in the slightest, but waking up across from Oliver, even if my hips were sore from sleeping on the hard floor, with our fingers barely holding onto each other might have been enough to convince me that mornings weren't so bad.

It was the first Christmas I could remember when I woke up not dreading the day. Where I woke up with even an ounce of happiness. I wouldn't be seeing my family today, nor would I be receiving any gifts or doing anything Christmassy—aside from Oliver's family dinner—but none of that bothered me as I studied the man sleeping feet away from me.

How did we even get here?

A year ago, I hated his guts and thought for sure that he hated me too.

But he had been harboring feelings for me this entire time. And now, I was waking up on his floor on Christmas, to his sleeping form and our fingers intertwined.

I didn't know why it all ended up the way it did, but watching Oliver's peaceful face as he slept, oblivious to my inner turmoil, I found myself grateful for the series of events that led here.

My fingers moved on their own, skimming against his, and he inhaled, his eyes blinking open. I loved him in his thick, Clark Kent glasses, but this version of him, waking up with no glasses and the scruff of his beard just a little thicker...

I wouldn't mind waking up to that every day.

Holy poop on a stick. Where did that thought come from?

I had never been the type of person to envision a future with someone. I was always careful not to, but Oliver had me deep in fantasy land.

"Morning, love." His voice was hoarse from sleep, and my stomach did a thousand somersaults at the sound—not to mention him calling me *love*.

I smiled. "Morning, sleepyhead."

Oliver closed his eyes and smiled. Then he gripped the blanket beneath me and tugged. I let out a little yelp but then I was next to him, his arms wrapped around me, and one of my legs draped over his.

"That's better," he murmured, and my insides melted a little more as he nuzzled his head beneath my chin.

I like sleepy Oliver.

We laid like that for a long time, until the grumbles of our stomach and the need for coffee forced us to move and participate in being adults again. But before I could untangle myself from his embrace, Oliver squeezed me tight.

"Happy Christmas, darling," he said, his voice buzzing against my neck.

I whispered back, "Happy Christmas, Oliver."

A slow smile worked its way over my face at those words and the possibility that maybe, just maybe...

This might be a happy Christmas after all.

After a heavy dose of coffee and a light breakfast—err, I supposed it was lunch by that point—which Oliver prepared, he dropped me off at home to get ready for dinner with his parents tonight. I had expected to spend most of the day with him, but he said he had a project to work on and he'd pick me up later tonight.

I tried to ask him what *project* he could have on Christmas Day, but he only smirked and gave me a cryptic, "You'll see."

To keep my anxiety from getting the best of me, I did my best to stay busy. I showered, cleaned my apartment, and watched a Hallmark movie, trying to distract myself from tonight's dinner. I even texted Elsie to ask how things were going with her family, but too quickly I ran out of things to keep me preoccupied. It was a valiant effort, but by the time he arrived, and I climbed in the Jeep, my entire body was itching with anticipation and nerves. Oliver was quiet as he drove, his fingers tapping a fast rhythm against the steering wheel.

Oliver's parents' house was lit up like a Christmas tree when we pulled into the driveway. A weighted silence fell between us as he shut the car off, and we both stared at the bright, multicolored two-story house.

That tense silence lingered between us, crackling like the air before a lightning strike.

There was so much that could go wrong with this dinner.

We had practiced being "relationshippy" a fair amount, but I was still worried that his father would sniff out that I had been using Oliver this whole time to get to him. Part of me was scared that if his father saw through us, he would plant doubts in Oliver's mind about me, and then he'd walk away from me for good.

His dad had already proven how difficult he could be, which added even more stress to trying to convince him that Oliver and I were together. It was my fault that Oliver had lied to his father in the first place, and now that things had escalated between us, I didn't want to let him down.

Never mind the fact that I needed his dad to like me if I wanted any sort of leg-up in the contest.

It wasn't that I doubted my skills, but against the rest of the entrants—not to mention Oliver—I didn't know what my chances were. But I needed that prize money, which meant it was imperative for his dad to like me.

Although, prize money aside, the idea of winning was appealing to me less and less, especially with how much I enjoyed doing that engagement shoot with Oliver. It had put dangerous fantasies in my head about starting a photography business with him someday, which I had been quick to shut down. Oliver might have feelings for me, but I didn't think there was a chance that he'd ever be interested in something like *that*.

"Are you ready?" Oliver asked, breaking me from my thoughts.

"Are you?" I replied, unwilling to voice how nervous I was.

I wasn't worried about pretending to be a couple after spending Christmas Eve together. No, my nerves had more to do with Oliver's father and what ridiculous things might come out of *my* mouth if he was cruel to his son.

Suddenly, this fake dating went from being a good idea to having a whole lot of negative consequences should it all go downhill. The thought of losing Oliver after admitting I shared his feelings made my lungs squeeze until I couldn't breathe.

Warm fingers brushed the hair out of my face, lingering on my neck. "Maya?"

I forced a smile onto my face, not wanting him to see how terrified of losing him I was.

"Let's do this," I said through my smile, albeit half-heartedly.

Oliver studied my face for a moment before he unbuckled his seatbelt, and we climbed out of the Jeep. He put an arm around my shoulder as we trudged up the walkway to the front porch.

"Just be yourself, princess. My mum will love you."

I cocked my head. "And your dad?"

He gave a quiet snort. "Don't worry about what he thinks. His opinion doesn't matter."

I nodded, unable to say anything else when, in this scenario, it *did* matter.

"Just so you know, Maya," he added as we walked up the porch steps. "This isn't fake for me. It hasn't been for a long time. We might be putting on a show tonight, but everything I do is real."

Goosebumps covered my skin, and I reached onto my tippy toes to kiss him. Just before our lips touched, the front door opened.

"Ollie Bear!" a woman cried.

Then the heat from his body disappeared as a tall, slender woman pulled him into a tight hug. Her dark hair was meticulously curled, and she wore a red sweater over a pair of leggings. Though she was at least twenty years older than us, she didn't look a day over forty.

Ollie Bear? I would never let him live that one down.

When they pulled apart, Oliver turned his mom toward me with a smile. "Mum, I'd like you to meet my girlfriend, Maya." The way he called me his girlfriend had goosebumps rising on my skin.

His mom's smile was blinding as she turned and pulled me into her strong arms. "It's so nice to finally meet you, Maya. Oliver has told me so much about you."

I arched a brow at him over her shoulder and he gave me a sheepish smile.

"It's lovely to meet you too, Mrs. Lewis."

She let go of me, batting her hand through the air. "Oh, please call me Molly."

His mom was so different from Oliver's father that I wondered for a moment how the two of them had even ended up together.

"Come in, come in! Dinner is almost ready."

Oliver took my hand, squeezed it once, then tugged me inside. The scent of garlic overwhelmed me as I took off my coat and boots and followed Oliver into the living room.

A giant tank of a man lounged on the couch. The most serious expression I had ever seen was plastered on his face, his dark hair slicked back with far too much gel, and he wore a black business suit.

Who wears a suit to a family dinner?

When he spotted us, he pushed to his feet in one smooth movement and extended a hand to me, ignoring his son.

"You must be the girlfriend."

"She has a name," Oliver bit out, but his father brushed him off.

"I'm Leander Lewis."

I gripped his hand, squeezing it tighter than necessary, trying to show him I wasn't scared of him, even though I was shaking in my socks.

"I'm Maya." I mimicked his stern voice.

I had a strange stare-down with Oliver's father, and I lost track of how long we stood there, still shaking hands and glaring at each other, until Molly put us out of our misery by clearing her throat and giving a loud clap of her hands.

"Leander, come help me set the table so these two can get settled in."

He grunted, flicking a disdainful look at Oliver before he followed his wife.

For a second, neither of us moved or said anything. Then, in typical Maya fashion, I blurted, "That went well."

Oliver snorted, his full lips twitching against a smile as he wrapped his fingers around my bicep and pulled me toward him. He planted a soft kiss on my cheek. My eyes fluttered open as he pulled away, and when I met his gaze, everything I was feeling toward him reflected in his eyes.

I could get used to him looking at me like that.

But my stomach grew uneasy, a heavy weight building in my chest. While I had told Oliver I had feelings for him, I hadn't said those three words, and suddenly that felt like it was vastly important. Maybe it would circumvent whatever happened tonight—or at least lessen the blow.

I was about to pull him into the bathroom and tell him I loved him—yes, so romantic—when Molly popped back into the living room.

"Dinner is served!" she announced, waving her hand toward the formal dining room.

I swallowed down the words as Oliver's fingers intertwined with mine and he led me to the table.

One would have thought that she had planned a dinner for twenty people. The long, wooden table was decked out in poinsettia and pine centerpieces, candles flickering away between them. A huge roasted duck was set on one end, surrounded by various vegetable casseroles, potatoes, bottles of wine, sparkling juice, and a pitcher of water.

"This looks incredible, Molly," I said, and she lit up from head to toe.

"Let's sit." Leander's gruff voice rang out. His chair squealed against the floor as he pulled it out and sank into it.

Molly deflated a bit, and Oliver was quick to step in,

giving his mom a side hug, and murmured something in her ear that brought that smile right back.

The rest of us sat down, and Molly started passing dishes around and we each helped ourselves. Minutes passed in silence as we ate, the only sound the grating of knives on porcelain. The food was amazing, perfectly seasoned and cooked, and Oliver and I were quick to tell her how delicious everything was.

Neither of us missed the grumpy way Leander sat there, sawing through his duck and shoving it into his mouth. He didn't compliment his wife on a good meal, nor did he offer any sort of conversation. Molly kept glancing at him, as if she were waiting for his approval or reassurance, but he sat there in moody silence, and she shrunk a little more as each minute passed.

I raised a questioning brow at Oliver, and he gave a half-hearted shrug and a minuscule shake of his head as if to say, *That's just my father. This isn't anything new.*

Gears started turning in my head and the urge to meddle rose to the surface. If Elsie were here, she'd tell me to just leave them be, to think of the contest and not poke the bear, but at the moment the contest was the furthest thing from my mind, and Leander needed to be poked. Preferably with a cattle prod.

I took a sip of water and cleared my throat. "Mr. Lewis," I began, and both Oliver and Molly perked up, looking at me with wide eyes. "Do you dislike roasted duck?" I nodded toward his plate where he'd eaten every last piece. If I hadn't watched him eat, I would've assumed he had licked the plate clean.

His lips turned down into a deep scowl that rivaled Grumpy Cat's. "No."

I plastered a pleasant smile on my face. "Well, if you liked it so much, don't you think you should give compliments to the chef?"

Oliver tensed beside me. Molly continued to stare at me with wide eyes, her cheeks turning pink.

"My wife knows I like her food," Leander growled, glaring at me.

I put my hands up in fake surrender. "I'm simply saying, sometimes it's nice to be told when the hard work we do is appreciated. My Aunt Maggie always said, 'please and thank you goes a long way in showing someone you appreciate them.'"

Leander's glare could've caused glass to shatter, but I kept a close-lipped smile on my face. Infinite seconds passed as we stared each other down before, to my surprise, he eyed his wife and mumbled, "it's a lovely meal."

Molly's cheeks reddened further as she stared at her husband in shock.

"Was that so hard, Mr. Lewis?" *Shut up, Maya!* I needed to quit while I was ahead, but my big mouth wouldn't be quiet.

Oliver's hand found my knee beneath the table and gave it a gentle squeeze.

A cold, calculating gleam entered Leander's eyes as

he stared me down. His gaze flicked from me to Oliver, back and forth several times before he sat back in his chair.

"Oliver tells me you like taking pictures," he said as he crossed his arms.

I swallowed, trying not to show my irritation at the way he said, "taking pictures."

"I do." Was he going to belittle me now like he did Oliver?

"Dad—"

Leander held up a hand, silencing him. "I heard good things about the engagement shoot the two of you did last week." Leander cocked his head. "The couple was quite pleased. Though, they seemed to be under the impression that Miss Maya was the one in charge."

Oliver didn't waste a second in coming to my defense. "I told Maya to take the lead at the shoot."

Leander's cold stare settled on his son. "And what right did you have to make that call?"

"Did you have any complaints from them?" Oliver asked instead.

His dad's eye twitched. "No."

"Then why does it matter? I made a good call, the couple was happy with their photos, and Maya got to do what she loves."

Leander turned his dark gaze back to me. "You want to be a photographer." It wasn't a question.

I could've word vomited all the reasons why I loved

photography, all the visions I had for the future, and how much I enjoyed taking photos with Oliver at my side, but I had a feeling that Leander wasn't interested in any of that. There was a sly look in his eyes, and I would bet money that the more I said, the more he would use and twist against me.

This man didn't care about my hopes and dreams for the future. The only man in the room who did was Oliver.

"Yes," I answered.

"And did you know that I am an owner of one of the largest photography agencies in all of England?" His voice was smug, full of sinister pride.

"Yes, I'm aware."

"Maya," Leander crooned, and I did not like the sound of my name in *his* accent at all. "Did you know that I am one of the judges for the *Rising Star Photography Contest?*"

The blood drained from my face, down my limbs, and pooled in my toes. *Uh-oh.*

When I didn't answer, his grin widened.

Then his gaze snapped to Oliver.

"When you mentioned your *girlfriend*, I did some checking up on her," Leander said to him.

Then my heart stopped.

"Did you know that she entered the competition?"

26

Maya

Oliver's hand tightened on my knee, but his expression remained blank.

Tears burned at the back of my eyes. After all this, all the hatred and bantering turned to love and real feelings, Leander Lewis was about to squash any chance with Oliver I had.

Oliver would never want to be with me after this. He would leave me. Just like everyone else. And I had no one to blame but myself.

I should've been honest. I should've told him the moment I started feeling something more for him.

My heart squeezed in my chest, aching something fierce. I had fought so hard against my growing feelings for Oliver, and yet I couldn't keep them away, couldn't help falling for him. And now that I had taken the risk, I would lose him.

I couldn't stand the thought of Oliver thinking I was like his cruel father—using him to get ahead. But in the end, that's what I tried to do, wasn't it? Now that I had Oliver, I wished I could go back in time and make a different decision. Maybe I wouldn't have entered the contest at all, or perhaps I would have never offered to be his girlfriend for Christmas.

But if I hadn't made those choices, would we have ever ended up here? Would I have ever come to care for him this much? Would we have gone to the tree farm, or gotten stuck in a blizzard, or had dinner with my family? My heart gave a lurch at the thought of Oliver missing from any of those memories. His presence made them special; one of a kind.

I clenched my hands into fists in my lap, frustrated that I couldn't read him. I didn't know which would be worse; seeing his face contorted in anger or continuing this blank expression that hid all his thoughts from me.

Would he call me out in front of his parents now? Would he yell at me and walk out the door, never looking back at the girl who used him?

"As a matter of fact, Dad, I did know," Oliver announced, shattering my thoughts.

He...knew?

I gaped at him, and even Leander blinked in surprise.

How was that possible? I never told him, and I did my best to keep Elsie and Jameson from ruining the secret.

He *knew* and still wanted to fake date and spend time with me? Why? I would have expected him to be furious with me. I was surprised he hadn't already walked out of his parents' house, leaving me behind for good.

My heart was a war horse in my chest, threatening to burst from my skin. I couldn't get enough air into my lungs; the colors around me dulled to muted colors.

"I beg your pardon?" his dad said, yanking me back to reality.

Oliver looked at me then and winked—wait, why did he wink?—and tugged my chair so it was touching his, and looped his arm around my shoulders, tugging me as close as possible.

"I already knew that Maya had entered the competition."

What was he playing at?

And why didn't he look angry? Did he not understand that I had used him?

"Why do you think I had her lead that engagement shoot?" He paused to let his words settle. "I knew that as soon as you saw Maya's entry, you'd discount her to get back at me because heaven forbid your son is with someone who makes him happy. But I also knew that if she did well, and the couple loved her, that you wouldn't be able to write her off. You'd have to pay attention to her and give her a chance. Maya is a brilliant photographer, and her photos deserve to be considered."

Leander's face turned bright red. "I didn't spend all these years helping you and honing your skill for you to throw it away on some American girl!"

Oliver laughed, though the sound was void of even a shred of humor.

"Helping me?" he scoffed. "No, you've been *using* me, Dad. The moment you first saw my ability with a camera, you've used it to further your own career. You don't care about me and what *I* want. You only care about the money and exposure I bring your company. I've had my fill of what *you* think being a photographer means. I never even wanted to enter the contest! I only did it so that maybe for once in my life you wouldn't look at me with disappointment in your eyes. But I don't want to win, especially if it's because of you. I'd rather bow out gracefully than spend another day working for you."

Oliver's hand trembled where it rested on my knee. This couldn't have been easy for him—standing up to his father. I put my hand over his, hoping to infuse more strength into him; letting him know I was supporting him, no matter what.

But then a slithering kernel of doubt began wriggling through my mind. Yes, Oliver was standing up to his dad, but what if it *was* only faking? What if he was *actually* furious with me, but he didn't want anyone to know? When we left their house, would he pull away from me, and tell me he never wanted to see me again?

I didn't know what was real or fake anymore and my insides were twisted, my limbs heavy.

Leander's cheeks were the color of beets. Molly stretched out a hand to him, likely trying to calm her husband, but he moved out of her reach, shrugging her off. Sympathy filled my veins as I watched the way she shrunk back in her chair, her shoulders curling forward as she ducked her head.

The sight reminded me of when Elsie had dated her scumbag ex, Ben. He treated her similarly to how Leander was treating Molly. Elsie had become a ghost of her true self around him, and it was the most satisfying day ever when she dumped his sorry butt.

I had a feeling that I understood why Molly lived in the States, away from him, for half the year now. I didn't blame her one bit.

I marveled for a moment at how wonderful Oliver was after seeing the horrible person his dad was. How had he turned out so amazing when his example was so awful? Molly must have done a great deal to counteract his terribleness.

Leander sputtered, trying to come up with something to say. I was certain that Oliver had never spoken to him in such a way, and now his father had no clue how to proceed.

He straightened in his chair and put two fists on either side of his empty plate. "How dare you? I should disqualify you right this minute!"

I held my breath as I waited for Oliver's response. I was confident in my photography skills, especially after how well that engagement shoot had gone, but Oliver had beat me over and over in our class last year. It had put enough doubt in my head for me to think that, if it came down to Oliver and me, he would win.

And I needed that prize money. But, even so, I loved Meridel. It was home, and I didn't want to be forced to leave, but if I didn't win that prize money, I might not have another option.

"No need," Oliver said, cutting through my anxiety. "I withdraw."

"Oliver—" I began but his hand moved higher on my leg, his fingers pressing into my skin, and my breath caught in my throat.

"You really think this girl has a chance against all the other entrants?" his father snapped, not even bothering to look at me while he insulted me.

Oliver didn't hesitate at all. "Absolutely."

"You're a blasted fool!"

"Leander—" Molly tried to calm him, but he shrugged her off again.

His utter dismissal of his wife had me seeing red.

"I didn't pay that pitiful college all that money to get you in that magazine just for you to throw away your big chance." Spittle sat on his lips, his face morphing from red to purple in his anger.

"You...what?" Oliver breathed. My own mouth was

hanging open too. "You paid off the community college?"

Leander straightened, clearly not expecting Oliver to question him. "You needed to win that spread in the *Iowa Artist Gazette*. Look at all the clients you picked up here in the States because of it! You're helping L.L. & Co spread internationally, just like we wanted. That wouldn't have happened if some girl had won instead," he spat, throwing a dismissive hand at me.

Oliver looked dumbfounded; his eyes wide as he gaped at his father. For a split second, the thought crossed my mind that perhaps Oliver had known what his father had done the entire time and was playing dumb. But the shock on his face told me that was false. Oliver had no idea just how scummy his father was.

And that meant...Oliver didn't beat me. I *could've* won had Leander not paid off our college. I was a finalist, after all. Just the thought of that had the shackles of doubt and insecurity crack and break off, and a surge of renewed confidence flooded through me.

But then Leander turned his dark gaze on me.

"Did you know, *girl*, that fraternizing with a judge's family in an attempt to gain favor in the competition is against the rules?"

I opened my mouth, but no words would come out.

"I should disqualify you right now. Then what use would you have for my son?"

His words had my heart stuttering, but for a different reason than I expected, and it sent a wave of shock through me.

As much as I needed that money, the thought of no longer worrying about the contest, of feeling guilty about using Oliver, and fighting the doubt that I could ever win, was enough for me to push to my feet.

I threw my napkin onto my plate and repeated Oliver's earlier sentiment. "No need, Mr. Lewis. I'm withdrawing from the competition too. Your son is incredible, brilliant, and a better man than you could ever hope to be. You'd see that if you ever bothered to have an actual conversation with him rather than belittling and berating him all the time."

Watching Leander's mouth fall open, his eyes widening at the audacity of my words, filled me with immense satisfaction.

"Thank you for dinner, Molly. Everything was delicious," I offered, putting a hand on her shoulder.

And then I stalked to the front door as the room went deathly silent, somehow keeping my fingers from shaking as I buttoned my coat and pulled on my boots before stomping outside, leaving the Lewis family gaping after me.

27

Oliver

"You're just going to let her talk to me like that?"

My father shouted at me when Maya was gone.

Pride mixed with an indescribable surge of love flooded through me over how she not only stood up for herself but defended me as well.

I smirked at my father. "Yes." And I'd let her do it over and over again if she wanted.

My father's face turned the color of purple bruises. Spittle peppered his lips as he fought for something to say, but, for the first time in his life, he must have been speechless because he didn't say a word.

I had no idea that he'd paid off the community college, and the knowledge burned through my veins, forcing my hands into tight fists. I couldn't believe my father. To me, that was the final nail in the coffin. I was done with him. I wouldn't let him use me to further his business anymore.

I pushed to my feet. I needed to go after Maya.

I saw it in her eyes. She was afraid I was angry with her for not telling me about the contest. I had lied before. I hadn't known she entered, at least not for certain, though, I had put the pieces together between the flyer in her bedroom and through conversation at Friendsmas with Maya's family.

No, I wasn't mad—not at her. Maybe I should've been more upset that she had been using me, but if I thought about it, I had used her too. And even if I wanted to be angry—I couldn't. I was too crazy about her.

I never wanted to enter in the first place and had considered withdrawing even before now.

I hated the idea that she might think I was angry with her. Did she expect me to come outside, finding her shivering in the cold, and yell at her for deceiving me? Because I would never do that. Sure, I wished she would have been honest with me, but I wasn't mad. In fact, if I had known, I would have withdrawn sooner, especially knowing the lengths my father was willing to go to make sure I won.

The fact that she was afraid I was upset told me something very important too: Maya cared what I thought.

The thought alone had me planting a kiss on my mum's cheek and saying a quiet thank you for dinner along with a "Happy Christmas."

Before I raced out into the cold night after the girl who had stolen my heart, I called over my shoulder to my father, "Oh, and that indefinite break I've been taking from the company? It's now permanent. I quit."

Snowflakes drifted down from the sky, shining like silver stars in the moonlight peeking through the clouds. The cold nipped at my nose and fingers, but the sensation disappeared as I rounded the corner.

Maya was pacing back and forth next to my Jeep. She was muttering something to herself, but it was too quiet for me to make out.

I couldn't help the smile that spread over my face as I watched her. Her hands were stuffed deep into her pockets, her shoulders hunched against the cold, her light curls sticking out of the beanie she must have stolen from my car. A surge of pleasure coursed through my body at the sight of her wearing something of mine.

When Maya noticed me standing there, she jerked to a stop, her eyes glistening in the moonlight.

"I'm sorry," she blurted. One errant tear slipped down her cheek. The sight of it had my heart cracking in two and my feet moving forward until I was close enough to wipe it away.

"You have nothing to be sorry for."

Her brows lowered. "What?" Another tear slipped down her face, and I was quick to stop it in its tracks.

"You have nothing to be sorry for, Maya," I repeated, enunciating each word.

"You…you're not mad?"

I quirked a brow. "Do you want me to be?"

She opened and closed her mouth. "Well, no, but…" Her face scrunched up in confusion. "I only agreed to be your fake girlfriend to gain an advantage in the photography contest through your dad."

I huffed a laugh, the breath clouding in the air between us.

"I saw the flyer in your bedroom the night of Friends-mas and I put the pieces together. It never mattered to me, darling."

Wide blue eyes blinked at me. "But I was *using* you."

"Technically, I was using you too. Fake girlfriend, remember?"

Maya snorted, a small smile cracking the sad expression on her face, but then she sobered and tried again.

"But…the only reason I agreed to fake date was to get to your dad. I didn't do it out of the goodness of my heart or to genuinely help you. I don't understand why you're not upset." She paused, swallowing. "Why aren't you mad? Why aren't you telling me you never want to see me again?"

My heart cracked further.

"Maya..." I pressed a kiss to her forehead before tilting her chin up so our gazes were locked together. "That may have been how we started, but you know things have been real between us for a while. It doesn't matter how it began as long as in the end, we're together. I'm *not* angry, and I'm *not* leaving."

She blinked at me. "After all of this, you still want to be with me? You still—"

"Love you? More than you can fathom, princess."

Maya gaped at me, her breath shuddering in the cold air. It was the first time I had said those words, and I meant them with all my heart. I hoped they would put her fears to rest for good.

"I'm not going anywhere, Maya. Unless you tell me to leave, I'm staying wherever you are. You may not be ready to say those words yet, but I know how you feel about me." I put her hand over my heart. "I feel it."

Maya's throat bobbed as she swallowed.

"I'm staying here, Maya," I reaffirmed. "With you."

Her lips turned down at the corners. "But what if I have to leave Meridel?"

"Why would you need to leave?"

She sighed before speaking so fast, I had to concentrate to understand everything coming out of her mouth. "I have a lot of debt, Oliver. I didn't have the cash for those photography classes or the lens I had to buy, and waitressing doesn't pay enough money to live off *and* pay down my debt. I entered that contest because of the prize money. If I had won, I would have been able to pay everything off. But now that I withdrew, I'm back to square one."

A stray tear escaped the corner of her eye. "I've tried for so long to make photography a career in Meridel, and it's just too small. I can't grow here. I don't have enough connections, and there aren't enough people in this small town to need or be able to afford enough photoshoots to keep me afloat. Now that the prize money is out of the picture, I'm going to have to consider leaving. Head somewhere where I have more of a chance at success, or..." She paused and let out a long breath. "Or seriously consider giving up on photography altogether and finding something else to do."

The thought of Maya no longer behind a camera made my heart throb. She was made for it. No...I couldn't let her give up. Not when I might have had the power to help.

Though she was upset and discouraged about this, hope flared in my heart. From the first moment at that engagement shoot days ago, Maya had proven how talented she was, and how focused she could be, and deserved so much more than what she had been able to do thus far.

Her photos were full of life, and the world needed more of them.

I hadn't dared to entertain the idea I had back then,

but now that things had changed, I wondered if she'd be more open to the idea.

"Answer me this, Maya. Money aside, do you want to leave Meridel?"

"No."

"And if you had more opportunities for photoshoots, would that enable you to stay?"

"What are you talking about, Oliver? I just said—"

I put a finger to her lips. "What if I had an idea that allowed you to stay here, *and* do what you love?"

Her eyes narrowed. "And how would that be possible?"

"What if…" I hesitated. Why was I nervous to tell her my dream? "What if *we* started a business together? I have a lot of connections and previous clients that would jump at the chance to work with me again thanks to the *Iowa Artist Gazette*. We could do shoots together, and you can keep all the money until your debt is paid off. I have enough saved to float for a while."

Maya blinked repeatedly like I had spoken in a foreign language, and she was trying to piece my words together one by one. Finally, she said, "Are you serious, Oliver?"

"I've never been more serious in my life."

"But what about your job?"

"I quit."

Her eyes bulged. "When?"

I shrugged. "Before I came outside."

"Don't you think that's a big deal?"

I shook my head. "It's been a long time coming. I want to see what I'm capable of outside of my father's shadow." I ran my thumb over her cheek. "I want to see what *we're* capable of, Maya. Say you'll at least think about it."

"But...you're from England. Are you saying you'd move to Meridel permanently?"

"Turns out I have a very compelling reason to stay," I replied, running my fingers across her cheek, down her neck. "*You* are what I want. *This* is what I want. Having a life here with you means gaining all the things I never dared to dream of."

I brushed my lips across hers. "I want *you*, Maya. As long as you're here, there's nowhere in this world I'd rather be."

She returned the kiss, her lips hot against mine as her hands wrapped around my neck, my own pressing into her back, pulling her as close as possible.

How did I get so lucky to be standing here, holding this woman? A year ago, I had the world's biggest crush on her, but the hate in her eyes when she looked at me always kept me far away from her. But now the world had twisted on its axis, and she was somehow in my arms, with her lips against mine.

She'd been through so much in her life, so much loss and heartache, and heck, so had I. Other men might have shied away from her, not wanting to touch those kinds of issues, wanting something simpler—easier.

But those men were all cowards.

And none of them deserved Maya Beck.

I would fight those demons of doubt and slay that dragon of fear that kept her afraid that everyone would leave her.

I would do whatever it took for her to see the amazing person I saw when I looked at her. Calling her princess was a joke at first, but she was every bit as special and important as a true princess to me.

When we pulled apart, I pressed a light kiss to the tip of her nose which was bright red from the cold. She rested her forehead against mine.

"I'm sorry this was such an awful Christmas dinner," I said, taking her hands in mine. "How about I make it up to you?"

My heart started thundering but I had never been so sure of anything in my life.

"You don't need to make it up—"

I silenced her with a look.

She sighed. "How?"

I grinned. "I thought you'd never ask. Come with me."

I laced our fingers together, tugging her down the icy sidewalk that led to a small park at the end of the road. She clung to me for dear life, trying not to slip and slide over the slick concrete.

"Where are we going?"

I gave her a mischievous grin. "You'll see."

Maya narrowed her eyes. "It's Christmas. Everything

is closed, Oliver."

I smirked. "Do you trust me?"

Part of me expected her to say no, so it was a surprise when she nodded.

"Where are we going?" she repeated.

I threw her a small smile. "Even when things seem grim, there's always some Christmas magic somewhere. You just have to know where to look."

28

Maya

Oliver's hand was a mini fire around mine despite the snow falling around us as we walked down the sidewalk. There were no streetlights around, so we were forced to rely on the moonlight peeking through the clouds to see where we were going.

At least until we got to the end of the sidewalk that brought us to a little park with a swing set and two slides.

On the other side, lit up like—well, like a Christmas tree—was a large evergreen covered in lights. It was the largest out of all the surrounding ones, and as Oliver tugged me closer, I noticed there were tinsel garlands wrapped around the boughs. I giggled to myself when I saw they only went halfway up the tree, as if whoever decorated it couldn't reach that far.

Oliver stopped next to the tree, and I raised my eyebrows in question.

"Is this the project you had to do earlier today?" I asked.

His smile nearly stopped my heart, and he nodded. "Close your eyes, darling."

I wasn't fond of being told what to do, but when he said it in that husky voice and tacked on *that* pet name… *Honey, I'll do whatever you want me to.*

I closed my eyes and the snow crunched beneath his footsteps as he went…somewhere.

Oliver started whistling—a song from Mario Kart of all things—and I fought the urge to open my eyes and peek at what he was doing.

As if sensing it, he crooned, "Don't you dare look, princess. I'm almost done."

"Done with what?"

"You'll see."

I forced myself to focus on the soft brush of snow-flakes hitting my skin so I wouldn't be tempted to open my eyes. After another couple of minutes, hot lips pressed against my forehead.

"Okay, you can look now." His voice shook, just a little.

When I opened my eyes, I had to cover my mouth to hold in a gasp.

Laying on the snow in front of the lit-up evergreen were dozens—no, hundreds—of rose petals. I took a step back, then another, to read what they spelled.

"'Real girlfriend?'" I read aloud.

Oliver cleared his throat and I turned to find him on one knee behind me.

This time I couldn't contain my gasp.

His answering smile had my heart stuttering. "Don't worry, I'm not proposing, princess." His grin stretched wider. "Not yet, anyway."

"Then why are you on one knee?"

"I wanted you to understand how serious I am about this—about us." His breath clouded in the air as he blew it out. "I'm crazy about you, Maya, and I don't need to tell you again that I have been for a long, long time."

He stood, taking my hands in his. "But I want you, Maya. I want you to be my *real* girlfriend. Enough of the faking and facade. I want you by my side, holding my hand. I want to be a part of making your dreams come true. I don't want to hold you back—I want to launch you forward. Whatever that looks like."

Oliver raised my hand to kiss the back of it. "I want a future with you, Maya, and this is the first step. Will you be my girlfriend? My *real* girlfriend?"

The funny thing was, a few weeks ago I would have said no. I would have laughed in his face and walked away, terrified to let him get any closer for fear of him leaving me.

But standing here now, seeing the way he looked at me, feeling his hands in mine...I couldn't even fathom a world without Oliver Lewis in it.

Nor did I want one.

I loved that he wasn't rushing me and that he wanted me to chase my dreams and stay by my side the entire time.

I never dreamed I'd find such a love—such a man.

I leaned forward onto my toes, pressing a soft kiss to his lips.

"Yes, Oliver. I'd love to be your girlfriend."

His eyes lit up, brighter than the tree behind me. Unable to stand being apart any longer, I leaped into his embrace, wrapping my arms around his neck and legs around his hips. Oliver didn't miss a beat, holding me tight.

"See? Christmas magic *does* exist," he said, looking up at me with the sweetest smile.

I returned the smile, pressing my lips to his. Then I pulled back, putting a hand to his cheek. With a shake of my head, I said, "No, this isn't Christmas magic…" My fingers tightened on the back of his neck, his blue eyes piercing into mine.

"This is *our* magic, Oliver. And it's the best kind."

EPILOGUE

Maya

Six Months Later

"I can't believe this is happening," Elsie muttered, making me laugh.

"What?" I asked, eyeing her simple sage green dress, a small bouquet of flowers in her hand.

Elsie fixed me with a *look*. "You're getting married before I am."

I rolled my eyes. "It's not my fault that you're taking forever with the wedding plans." I fought the urge to stick my tongue out at her.

"Yeah, but you didn't even plan a wedding, Maya. You're *eloping*."

The way she said the word made it sound dirty.

But it wasn't. This was what Oliver and I had chosen. We didn't want a big wedding, and instead wanted to celebrate with the people closest to us.

Plus, with me and Oliver's photography business exploding over the past few months and all the resulting traveling we'd been doing, neither of us had the time or energy to plan a big, elaborate wedding.

This made sense for us.

"It's what we want, Els," I said, smiling at my best friend. "Are you actually upset?"

Elsie's smile was bright as she grinned at me. "Of course not, Maya. I'm so happy for you." She pulled me into a hug, squeezing the living daylights out of my lungs.

"Though, technically," Emma said as she came around the corner in a green dress of her own, breaking up our hug, "can it be called eloping since we're still in Meridel?" She cast an anxious look around. Emma had been on edge ever since we told her where the ceremony would be held.

I stuck my tongue out at her. "Well, it's sudden and last minute, and only possible because the Walker family allowed us to use the gazebo on their property for the ceremony, and only you two, Jameson, Aunt Maggie, and Molly will be here, so I'd consider it eloping."

She was clearly nervous about being here. She had a lot of memories that haunted her, but I wasn't about to let it ruin my day.

I let out a long shaky breath, smoothing down the white, satin dress I was wearing.

Oliver and I were getting married.

It was just shy of six months since he had asked me to be his girlfriend beneath the lights of that evergreen tree.

So much had happened in such a short time.

We started our photography business together, and any anxiety I had about it was quickly erased. Thanks to his endless connections, our business grew in the blink of an eye, way faster than either of us expected, and we were so busy that we were already booked halfway through next year.

I never imagined this could be my reality, going from enemies to owning a business together, but the fact that I got to do what I loved next to the man I loved made it even more special.

Plus, it didn't hurt that within a few months, my debt was paid off, removing that weight from my shoulders. For the first time in almost two years, I could breathe— and it was all thanks to the man I was about to marry.

Since we both withdrew from *Rising Star*, we never learned who won, and frankly, neither of us cared. The way things turned out was so much better.

His dad went back to England, and we visited his mom often since she had decided to remain in Iowa full time.

"Are you ready?" Emma asked, grabbing her bouquet.

I smoothed down my dress once more before picking up a larger bundle of cream and blush themed flowers. It was full of poppies—my favorite—pink roses, baby's breath, and chrysanthemums. It was stunning and smelled like the first day of spring.

"I've never been more ready for anything in my life," I replied before following Elsie and Emma out to the field which held the gazebo where I would marry Oliver.

Someone must have given Jameson the signal because music started as soon as my feet hit the grass, and Elsie and Emma walked down the path ahead of me. Molly stood next to Oliver, and Aunt Maggie sat in a wheelchair next to the other girls.

Time sped up—like it always did around Oliver—as I walked down the rose petal covered grass toward the man in a tux standing under the gazebo.

His smile was like a secret meant only for me—full of joy and dreams.

A year ago, I would have laughed at the idea of getting married, let alone to Oliver Lewis.

I never imagined it was in the cards for me, but now I couldn't imagine anything else.

I came to a stop at the steps of the gazebo, and Oliver extended a hand to guide me up. His blue eyes shined as we came face to face at the top.

"You're breathtaking, darling."

My smile was automatic. "You don't look too bad yourself."

His smirk had my stomach tightening.

"Are we ready?" Jameson asked.

Since this wouldn't be a traditional wedding, we

didn't want to have to worry about finding someone to marry us—and when Jameson offered to take the little online course that allowed him to perform the ceremony, it felt like the perfect fit.

Jameson cleared his throat. "I didn't memorize this, you guys, and I don't promise it won't be cheesy."

I shrugged. "I like cheese."

Oliver's smile squeezed all the air from my lungs. "As do I."

I winked at Jameson. "Proceed with the cheese, Jam-Jam."

My cousin started talking—or should I say reading—but with Oliver staring at me like he was, I hardly heard any of it. When it was time to say our vows, I snapped out of the trance his gaze had put me under.

"Oliver," Jameson said, pulling a folded piece of paper from his coat pocket. "Your vows."

Oliver released my hands and unfolded the paper.

"Maya." His voice trembled, just the tiniest bit, and I took hold of his other hand.

"You are my love, my princess, and I can't imagine a world that doesn't have you in it. I never imagined that you'd give this Blasted Brit a chance, but I'm so very thankful that you did. You are my everything, Maya. I promise to love you from now until our last day. I promise to encourage you to chase your dreams and help you reach them however I can. I promise to always be there for you, no matter what comes our way."

He paused, tears brimming in his eyes. He took a deep breath and continued. "I promise, my love, to find new magic—to create new magic—each day. Because our love is magic, and it is the very best kind."

The memory of my own words last Christmas flashed through my mind.

"Oliver, do you take Maya to be your lawfully wedded wife?" Jameson asked, handing him a ring.

Oliver slipped it on my finger. "I do."

Jameson handed me my vows then.

Before I even opened my mouth, tears spilled out of my eyes. *How does anybody do this?*

Oliver wiped them away, holding back some of his own.

"Oliver," I croaked, trying to hold myself together enough to read the words I had written down. "I don't have a lot of fancy words to say, but I know that I love you with everything that I am. You brighten my days and sweeten my nights. Your arms are the one place I know I am safe. You make me happier than anyone has ever been able to, and I can't wait to spend the rest of my life with you. I promise to stand by your side, to love you, and create a life full of magic and joy and dreams and wonder. No matter what comes, we'll face it together because we're stronger together than we are apart. I love you, Oliver. Forever and for always."

Jameson cleared his throat, and I didn't miss the way he sniffled as he handed me the other ring. "Maya, do you take Oliver to be your lawfully wedded husband?"

I didn't hesitate as I slid the ring on his finger.

"I do."

Oliver's smile was brighter than the sun.

"Then by the power vested in me by the state of Iowa, I now pronounce you man and wife. Oliver, you may kiss your bride."

My husband wrapped his hands around my waist and tugged me toward him.

"Here's to a lifetime of magic, my love."

I put a hand to his cheek. "The very best kind."

And then he kissed me, which was magic in and of itself.

THE END

The Mistletoe Bluff
Playlist

15 songs

Like It's Christmas
Jonas Brothers

All You Need to Know
Gryffin, SLANDER, Calle Lehmann

First Time
Seven Lions, SLANDER, Dylan Matthew

Wish List
Colin & Caroline

Anywhere For You
John Martin

Me Without You
Havelin

Winter Wonderland
Michael Bublé

i don't wanna know
Goldhouse, Mokita

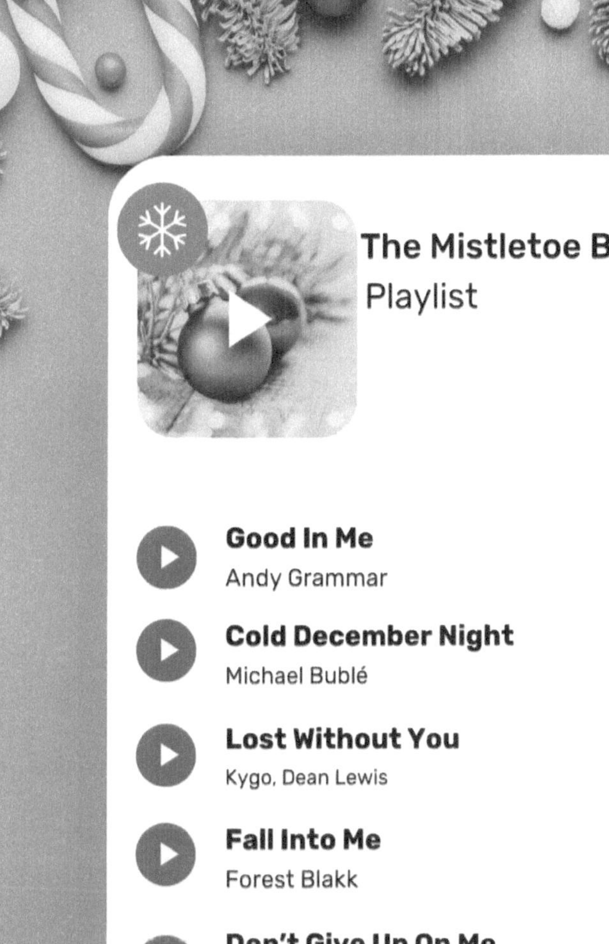

The Mistletoe Bluff
Playlist
Good In Me
Andy Grammar
Cold December Night
Michael Bublé
Lost Without You
Kygo, Dean Lewis
Fall Into Me
Forest Blakk
Don't Give Up On Me
Andy Grammar
Perfect (Acoustic)
Ed Sheeran
White Christmas
Bing Crosby, Pentatonix, London Symphony Orchestra

Did you love The Mistletoe Bluff?

Please consider leaving a review on Amazon to help other readers discover the magic of Maya and Oliver's story too!

Acknowledgements

I have always wanted to write a Christmas book. There's just something about cozy rom-coms with Christmas vibes that feels extra comforting and special around the holidays. *The Mistletoe Bluff* not only is my dream coming true, but it has some of my all-time favorite tropes which made it SO fun to write. This was probably one of the easiest books I've written—not that writing a book is ever easy. But Maya and Oliver's story was just waiting to be told, and I sincerely hope you enjoyed it!

Writing and publishing a book is not for the faint of heart, and there are several people I could not have done this without.

Thanks be to God—for His never-ending faithfulness throughout this entire process. Whether I needed peace or provision, He always came through. He never failed. I'm so thankful for this gift that He has given me, and may He get all the glory from this book. I would not be where I am without Him.

To my husband, Cody—Thank you for pushing me to keep dreaming, and reminding me that the doubts and fears in my head are all lies to keep my stories away from those who need it.

To Brittany Cox—you are the light in the doubt-filled darkness of my mind, and I don't think I could keep writing books without your constant encouragement, and confidence in my ability. Thank you for always believing in me, even when you weren't too sure about the rom-com genre lol. Your friendship is irreplaceable and I'm so thankful to have you in my life.

To The Authorteers—I am so blessed to have found writer buddies like you. Thank you for your constant support, for talking me off many cliffs, and for helping me stay somewhat sane (is there really true sanity in being an author?)

To Vanessa, Tiffany, Natalia, Rachel, and Angelica—thank you for beta reading the scary draft of my book, for all your constructive criticism, as well as your encouragement. It's terrifying having readers see my story for the first time, but your feedback has helped me make *The Mistletoe Bluff* what it is. Y'all are the best!

To all my author/bookstagram friends—I'm so thankful for each of you! Your excitement, encouragement, and every like, comment, and share mean so much to me. I feel so blessed every day to have found a community of people who are so supportive and that cheer me on.

To Katie, my editor—thank you for all the work you put into editing my book and encouraging me along the way. Your excitement and enthusiasm, along with your attention to detail, truly pushed me to keep going, and I don't think I can express how much it meant to me. You helped me make this story what it is, and it never would have been possible without you.

And to my readers—I am beyond honored that you chose to give me a chance and pick up one of my books. I hope this story made you smile and reminds you of both the magic of Christmas and the magic of love. I hope you walk away from this book feeling uplifted, hopeful, and have a big old grin on your face. Thank you for giving *The Mistletoe Bluff* a chance. It means the absolute world.

THE
Love Chase

COMING SPRING 2024

Emma

I swear I could feel the ticking of my watch like a hammer against my wrist. The ceremony was lovely, and I was so immensely happy for my cousin and Oliver. However, the little fact that we were on *this* farm had my heart stuttering in my chest, threatening to rip from my body and jump into the pond over yonder.

Was that a tad dramatic? Perhaps. But I had vowed never to set foot on this farm again.

And yet here I was.

I glanced around again, for the umpteenth time. I couldn't help it.

It's not like I'd see *him* here. He left two years ago—me and all of Meridel—for some pipe dream in California.

Was I bitter about it?

Maybe just a little.

If it weren't for the rumor I had heard at Dina's that *he* was coming home, I wouldn't have been so high-strung about being here.

Dang flabbit. Why did his *family farm have the most romantic feel? Why couldn't it have been…anybody else?*

I took a deep breath, watching Maya and Oliver sway back and forth to a slow song under the gazebo. They hadn't wanted a big reception after the ceremony, but none of us were ready to leave once it was over. So, Jameson grabbed a Bluetooth speaker from his truck and set it up in the gazebo. The two couples had been dancing the night away for the past hour.

Which left me—single ol' me—alone.

I told myself I didn't care. I was perfectly content to be single. I didn't need a man.

Certainly not *him.*

Dang it. Why did my mind keep going back there?

Throat parched, I walked over to the cooler sitting in the shade next to the barn. I had just grabbed a Cherry Coke from the depths of the ice when the last voice I ever wanted to hear said my name.

"Emma?"

I stiffened, refusing to turn and acknowledge him.

"Nope," I said, popping my lips, and started walking away.

"Emma," he repeated.

"Nope. No. I'm not speaking to you." I squeezed

my eyes shut, which was probably a bad idea since I was walking as fast as my long legs would carry me.

Of course, those long legs were clumsy, and I tripped on a random hole in the ground, stumbling forward.

Warm hands grabbed my waist, keeping me from face-planting into the ground.

"Emma." The voice of my childhood best friend was so soft it was like a caress. An apology.

I squeezed my eyes against the memories flooding my mind. Running around the farm, watching the meteor showers on cloudless nights, cow tipping—because duh, we live in the middle of nowhere—and sharing our deepest darkest secrets.

A light laugh echoed in my ears that I was far too familiar with—one that made my heart do strange things in my chest.

"Walking is easier if you do it with your eyes open," he crooned in my ear. Goosebumps pebbled my skin.

I still refused to open my eyes.

"Em."

The voice sure was persistent. Clearly, I had been in the hot sun for too long. The stress of being here had my brain imagining things.

"No. This is a dream. You're not real. This is all stress-induced. A hallucination."

"I assure you, it's not."

I shook my head as though that would lessen the impact his voice was having on my heart.

"I thought you'd be happy to see me."

At this, my eyes snapped open, and I turned to glare at the man I never expected to see again.

Liam hadn't changed at all. He still kept his light hair short, spiked just a little at the front that reminded me of 90's boy bands. His vintage band T-shirt hugged his muscles, and his cowboy boots were mud-crusted as though he just came from feeding the cows. His greenish gray eyes were familiar in a way I wished they weren't—especially because I had spent way too many years as a teenager pining over them.

But he never knew that. I'd never dared to tell him how I felt.

We had been best friends. Nothing more.

"What are you doing here, Liam?" I finally said with a sigh. "You're not supposed to be here."

"Last I checked, I am. I live here, remember?"

I gave another violent shake of my head. "No. You live in California. *Remember?* You left Meridel to follow your dreams."

Liam's smile was taunting, full of mischief.

Then he said the last words I wanted to hear from him. Words that held far too much promise and made my heart do horrendous little flips that I had worked so hard to quell over the last two years since he left.

Five little words that effectively tipped my world upside down.

"I moved back to Meridel."

If you loved The Mistletoe Bluff...

be sure to check out the first standalone in the series:

The Heart Shot!

Head to emilyschneiderwrites.com to check it out!

Don't Miss the Multi-Award-Winning Ash & Smoke Series!

When Kaida, a lifelong slave to her dragon master, Eklos, is stolen away by the Prince of Elysia, he reveals that she is not who she thinks she is.

Her long-awaited freedom will come at the cost of becoming what she despises and fighting to save what she never though she could love.

2021 Best Indie Book Award Fantasy Winner
2022 MN Author Project YA Fiction Winner

Kaida's greatest enemy wants revenge. His army is sweeping across the country, slaughtering every human in sight.

Now, Kaida and Prince Tarrin must raise an army to defeat the Remnant of the Lone Dragon. With the enemy on their heels, heartbreak and betrayal are hidden around every corner.

2022 Best Indie Book Award Dragon Fantasy Winner

War is coming and all hope seems lost.

Can Kaida and Tarrin finally overcome Eklos's tyranny in the war of Elysia's future? Or will their inner demons defeat them before the war has even begun?

Head to emilyschneiderwrites.com to check out the complete trilogy!

About the Author

Emily Schneider is a multi-award-winning author who grew up in Minnesota where she spent most of her life studying music and singing, which ironically has nothing to do with writing fantasy novels and rom-coms. While music had always been a passion, Emily could never get away from her love of reading and writing books full of dragons, Fae, monsters, magic, and romance. When she's not writing, you can find Emily chasing around her two dogs, Pixel and Frodo, playing Mario Kart with her husband, or watching The Lord of the Rings for the one-hundred-and-eleventh time.

emilyschneiderwrites.com

@emilyschneiderwrites